THE GOLDEN MAZE

THE GOLDEN MAZE

Hilary Wilde

CHIVERS
THORNDIKE

This Large Print book is published by BBC Audiobooks Ltd, Bath, England and by Thorndike Press®, Waterville, Maine, USA.

Published in 2006 in the U.K. by arrangement with the author.

Published in 2006 in the U.S. by arrangement with Juliet Burton Literary Agency.

U.K. Hardcover ISBN 1–4056–3783–8 (Chivers Large Print)
ISBN 13: 978 1 405 63783 1
U.K. Softcover   ISBN 1–4056–3784–6 (Camden Large Print)
ISBN 13: 978 1 405 63784 8
U.S. Softcover   ISBN 0–7862–8738–1 (British Favorites)

The text of this Large Print edition is unabridged.
Other aspects of the book may vary from the original edition.

Set in 16 pt. New Times Roman.

Printed in Great Britain on acid-free paper.

British Library Cataloguing in Publication Data available

Library of Congress Cataloging-in-Publication Data

Wilde, Hilary.
    The golden maze / by Hilary Wilde.
        p.   cm.
    "Thorndike Press large print British favorites."
    ISBN 0–7862–8738–1 (pbk. : alk. paper)
    1. Inheritance and succession—Fiction. 2. England—Fiction.
3. Large type books. I. Title.
PR6072.E735G65 2006
823'.914—dc22   2006009349

CHAPTER ONE

Cindy frowned as she gazed up at the names on the board, high up on the wall, that she could not see properly. She had almost run up from Ludgate Circus, hardly hearing the roar of traffic, for all she could think of was the *Castle.*

The castle of her dreams!

And now here she was to learn all about it and she couldn't even see which floor the solicitors were on!

'Having trouble?' A deep masculine voice interrupted her thoughts. Startled, she swung round and saw the man standing by her side. She couldn't see his face clearly, but he was tall, with broad shoulders, and blond hair. He towered above her.

'Why not wear glasses?' he asked, sounding amused. 'Then you could see.'

'I do usually.' She gave an excited little laugh, 'but I was in such a hurry to get here I forgot them. I mean, it isn't every day you inherit a castle!'

'A castle?' He sounded surprised, then paused before continuing: 'You've inherited a castle?'

The condescension in his voice irritated her, but she answered: 'Yes, a real castle . . .' then she corrected herself: 'At least it will be mine if

1

his son doesn't turn up.'

'His son? So there's a son.' For some odd reason, the man sounded more amused than ever, so Cindy frowned.

'It's quite simple. If the son can't be found after three years' searching, I'll inherit the castle.'

'If there's a son alive, where do you come into it?'

'Well, you see they don't know. I mean if the son is alive or not. It seems he quarrelled with his father years ago and walked out and—well, I suppose the father was sorry. Anyhow he left everything to his son, but if the son wasn't traced for three years, then it comes to me. I honestly don't know why.' Cindy shook her head thoughtfully, her long chestnut-brown hair swinging. 'I hardly knew him—Mr. Baxter, I mean. I was about seven when Mummy, who was a widow, met him and we were asked there for a holiday. She hated the quietness. I loved it . . .' Remembering, Cindy half-closed her eyes. 'It was absolutely super. A real castle! Of course I had the usual absurd dreams.' She laughed and then looked grave. 'They weren't just dreams at the time. I persuaded myself that I was a princess and that my so-called parents had found me in a dustbin and that one day, the truth would be discovered and I would live in the castle and it would be mine . . .' As she spoke, her voice rose excitedly. 'And now this . . . this has happened.'

'The son might turn up,' the stranger said dryly.

Cindy nodded. 'Of course he might, but they've been hunting for him for three years and the solicitor's letter said only three weeks were left of the search . . .'

'Where is this wonderful castle?'

'Cumberland—in the Lake District. I can just remember the lakes and the mountains and the . . .'

'Castle.' He gave a funny little laugh. 'How will you run it? Castles cost money, you know.'

Cindy tossed her head, her hair swinging. 'I'll find a way.' She twisted her hands together, her brown handbag hanging from her shoulder, her little oval face framed by the pale pink woollen cap. 'It's so wonderful, you see. I woke up this morning feeling . . . feeling so unhappy. So . . . well, rejected. No one cared for me. I was all alone, and then—then this letter came. I couldn't believe it. Uncle Robert—that's what he made me call him— hadn't forgotten me. He said he wanted the castle to go to someone who loved it as he did. Just think, he hadn't forgotten me all these years. Ever since I was seven.'

'How long ago is that? Eight years?'

Cindy's eyes blazed, for she hated this kind of joke. Just because she had a young look! Her cousins were always teasing her about it, too, just as they did about her miserable five

3

feet two inches height.

'I'm nineteen years and ten months,' she said with dignity as well as anger.

'Is that so? You don't look it. Well, I'm thirty-three and seven months.'

'Well, you . . .' she began indignantly, and stopped, having to laugh instead. 'I'm afraid I can't see you properly,' she admitted, and looked at her watch. 'Help! I must hurry and see the solicitor. I told my boss I'd be as quick as I could.'

'I thought you only got your letter this morning?'

'I did, but I rang my boss at once. He's always late at work himself, so I rang his home and he quite understood. He told me to be as quick as I could, so I must . . .'

'How can you have a castle in Cumberland and a job in London? Rather an expensive distance to commute,' the stranger said dryly.

Cindy laughed: 'Oh, I'll give up my job, of course. Could you tell me which floor Ayres & Bolton are on?'

'Certainly. Third floor. The lift's over there. Do you think you can reach the button . . .?'

Her face flamed. 'Of course I can,' she said angrily.

'Well, watch your way. You're moving in a golden maze.'

Even as she started to turn, she paused. 'A golden maze?' she repeated, puzzled.

He smiled. 'Dryden. "I think and think on things impossible, And love to wander in that golden maze".'

'Oh.' Cindy hesitated. 'You mean dreams. What's wrong with dreams?' she asked defiantly.

'Nothing—except that you get hurt when the balloons burst.'

'This one isn't going to,' she told him, and hurried to the lift.

Inside it, she wondered at herself. How could she have talked so easily to a complete stranger? Why? She must have bored him terribly. That was another thing her cousins were always telling her: that she talked too much. What must he think of her? she asked herself as the lift stopped and she hurried down the carpeted corridor to a door with the names Ayres & Bolton on it. *'Please walk in'*, she read underneath them.

Obeying, she went through a glass door that swung open as she touched it and a girl with blonde hair, piled high on her head, looked up.

'My name is Lucinda Preston,' Cindy said. 'I rang Mr. Ayres early this morning in reply to his letter.'

The girl smiled. 'Of course. Please sit down and I'll see if Mr. Ayres is ready.'

Cindy obeyed, looking round her curiously. It was all very modern and luxurious so it must be a reliable firm, she decided.

The girl returned. 'Mr. Ayres will see you

now. This way.'

Cindy followed her down the carpeted corridor and into a large room with an enormous picture window that showed St. Paul's Cathedral in all its dignified glory, but Cindy was looking at the lean, handsome man who came to meet her, holding out his hand. His hair was dark but greying at the temples, his eyes were dark too and he had a pleasant friendly smile. She liked him at once.

'How good of you to contact me so quickly,' he said, shaking her hand, leading her to a chair, then sitting opposite her on the other side of the large walnut desk. He ruffled through some papers and then looked up with a smile. 'You are Miss Lucinda Preston, daughter of the late Bartholomew Preston and of Winifred, his wife? You are, I understand, an only child? Your father died when you were very young and your mother when you were ten years old?'

Cindy nodded, her eyes misting. Would she ever forget the awful loneliness when her mother died? The knowledge that she was a nuisance to her cousins, and an unwelcome burden to their parents, for she had been tossed from one aunt and uncle to another, Maybe she had been stupidly sensitive, but she still inwardly squirmed at the memories of her older cousins' teasing. 'Goggly-eyed Cindy'; 'Tiny Cindy'; 'Brainless Cindy'. Her height had been a handicap, for they were all tall; all

6

bright at school, flowing effortlessly through exams while she, working like mad, just managed to squeeze past the final posts. That was why, as soon as she could, she had learned shorthand and typing, got herself a good job and a bed-sitter in Earls Court. Living sensibly, she had saved enough money to buy herself a car—small, grey and efficient. It made all the difference in the world to her life, for every weekend she could slip away to the quietness of the country she loved.

She realised with a shock that she hadn't been listening to the solicitor. Her cheeks hot, she apologised.

'I am sorry, I was thinking . . .'

He smiled. 'That's all right. I asked if you could remember Mr. Baxter.'

Cindy shook her head slowly. 'Not really. Just as a big man with a kind voice. I know he was a friend of Mummy's—they met somewhere and he asked us to visit him. I loved it, but Mum hated it, so we never went back again.'

'You loved it?'

Her eyes shining, Cindy nodded. 'It was super. The most exciting and romantic thing that ever happened to me. Living in a castle!' She sighed ecstatically.

Mr. Ayres smiled. 'It's not a real castle, you know. It's what is called a mock castle . . . built years after real castles were built.'

'It may be mock or real, but I remember it

7

as a castle. It looked just like one—with a drawbridge and a moat and vaults and . . .' Cindy stopped. 'I expect you've seen it.'

'No, I haven't. My uncle was alive at that time and Mr. Robert Baxter was his client.'

'I'll never forget it, ever. There were mountains and a great lake and then this lovely castle . . . Mummy had always read me fairy stories and, of course, I felt like a princess in her castle, waiting for my handsome prince to come.'

'It certainly made an impression on you.' Keith Ayres smiled. 'As I told you in my letter, Mr. Baxter never forgot your love of the place.'

'I can't understand how he could remember me all these years.' Cindy spread out her hands expressively.

'He was old and lonely. It was a pity about his son. Mr. Baxter was devoted to the boy. These family quarrels are sad things. Fathers so easily forget how they felt when they were sons.'

'Well, if you build up a big business, surely you're building it for your son, too?' Cindy asked. 'Not that that means the son must automatically follow on, of course.'

Keith Ayres smiled ruefully. 'It's so easy to judge. I'm not married, so can't talk from experience, but I'm building up this firm from the mess it was in when my uncle died, and I must confess, I'd like a son of mine to benefit

8

as a result of my hard work.'

'It's funny, isn't it, as you grow older everything seems to reverse,' Cindy began, and stopped abruptly. It was when she said stupid things like that that her cousins called her a bore. 'You . . . you haven't found Mr. Baxter's son?'

'No, but there are still three weeks . . .' Keith Ayres hesitated before continuing. 'Actually we fear he is dead. We traced him to Australia, then Canada, and finally South America. There was some turmoil there and he just vanished. We have advertised . . . are still advertising.' He frowned. 'Your mother didn't like the castle?'

'It wasn't that—it was the loneliness. Mummy liked people and bright lights and . . . and life, as she called it. I'm more like my dad, an introvert.'

Keith Ayres laughed. 'I'd hardly call you that. You can't remember anything about Mr. Baxter?'

Cindy looked round the luxurious office and half closed her eyes. 'What you said about a mock castle . . . that does seem to ring a bell.' She clapped her hands excitedly. 'I've got it! I remember how Mummy told me that. She said it wasn't a real castle and . . . and I remember crying and then . . .' Cindy frowned thoughtfully, her eyes narrowed. 'Yes, I am beginning to remember. This man I had to call Uncle Robert gave me a big white hankie and

9

said it would always be a real castle to him, and that made me awfully happy, because it was *his* castle, so he had to be right. It *was* real!'

Keith Ayres looked thoughtful. 'What you liked when you were seven years old may look different now, Miss Preston. Er . . . did your mother . . . er . . . I don't want to sound impertinent, but have you a private income?'

Looking surprised, Cindy shook her head. 'No, Mummy had an annuity which died with her. I lived with aunts and uncles and I got a job as soon as I could and . . . well, I'm not doing too badly. I have a car and . . .'

Keith Ayres smiled. 'Very commendable, Miss Preston, but I doubt if it would be enough to enable you . . .' He paused. 'Mr. Baxter was not a rich man when he died. Locals believed him to be wealthy, but he had many troubles financially as well as physically. I'm afraid after all the death duties and taxes, etc., there won't be much money left. The reason I wished to contact you before the three years was up was because, at the moment, you view this inheritance with romantic eyes, but it could become a pain in the neck. The castle is large and expensive to keep in repair. In addition there is a housekeeper and her son, the gardener, who have been there ten years. Efficient, I gather, but expecting and getting generous salaries. The estate pays this at the moment. You may find it advisable to sell the castle.'

Cindy's eyes widened in horror. 'Sell it? Sell the castle?'

Keith Ayres tried not to smile. 'Well, until I wrote to you you had forgotten it, so it can't mean all that much.'

'Oh, but it does, and I hadn't . . .' Cindy leaned forward, her hair swinging on either side of her face. 'It's always been a wonderful dream to me. If things got bad, I could cheer myself up by thinking of the castle that would one day be mine. It was a dream that had somehow come true, if you know what I mean?'

'Yes, I do, but all the same . . . Look, I think it would be a good idea for you to visit it as soon as possible, Miss Preston.'

Cindy's eyes brightened. 'I'd love to visit it.'

'Good. I suggest you talk things over with your boss and get a week off. Let me know the date you can go up to Cumberland and I'll arrange with Mrs. Stone—she's the housekeeper—to expect you. You can go by train or coach.'

'I'll drive up, I don't know that part of England, so it will be fun,' Cindy told him eagerly.

Keith Ayres hesitated. 'You're rather young to drive around alone.' He saw the frown on her face and hastily added, 'I was thinking if the car broke down, some of those roads in the Lake District in winter can be very isolated.

11

You have a friend who could go with you?'

It was Cindy's turn to hesitate. 'Yes,' she said slowly, which wasn't the whole truth but half of it. She had *friends* at the office, but the friendship ended at five o'clock each day. Somehow she wasn't one of them. She had found London lonely, but with the weekends in the country to look forward to, she had learned to live with loneliness.

'Good.' Keith Ayres stood up and smiled. 'Let me know which day you're free to go up to the castle and I'll contact Mrs. Stone.' He hesitated. 'I hope you won't be too disillusioned, Miss Preston.'

She shook hands with him at the door and her eyes were bright with excitement. 'I'm never disillusioned, Mr. Ayres.' she said gaily. 'Mummy used to say, when one door closes another opens. Something good always happens to me.'

Look at today, she told herself as she hurried down towards the large block of offices where she worked, she had woken up that morning, feeling depressed, dreading the hours at the office where she could see mirth mixed with sympathy in the girls' eyes because she had been dropped by Oliver Bentley. And then the letter had come! The letter that had opened a whole new exciting world for her.

Now as she hurried down the corridor in the office building, she smiled through the glass walls of the typing pool and waved to the girls gaily. She had the most wonderful news imaginable to tell them. What did Oliver matter after all? True, he was a charmer and she had enjoyed the two evenings he took her out. He had been attentive, kissing her . . . and then next day she had been cut dead by him and later, meeting in the canteen, he had paused by her side and said:

'It was nice knowing you, Cindy, but not half as nice as I'd hoped.'

One of the typists, close behind Cindy, had giggled. Cindy hadn't understood what Oliver meant, thinking it must be because she was— as her cousins had frequently told her—an awful bore. That she was a *nothing*. That no man with any sense would look at her! As Oliver hurried by, Maggie, the girl behind Cindy, had squeezed her arm.

'It's not your fault, Cindy, you're just not with it,' she said sympathetically, which had made it worse. But today . . . why, a castle was better than all the Olivers in the world put together!

As soon as Cindy had hung up her winter coat and little hat, carefully looked at her face and wondered why she looked so different, her cheeks flushed, her eyes shining, she hurried to her boss's office, her notebook in hand, half a dozen pencils ready.

'Well?' Patrick Jenkins looked up. A tall, lean man with reddish hair and green eyes, he was a hardworking boss whom most of the girls

13

disliked but whom Cindy enjoyed working for.

'I told you it was a castle!'

Patrick Jenkins grinned. 'You know, I was half asleep when you phoned this morning, and you should know by now that I can't think properly until twelve o'clock, so please tell me slowly and in detail what happened.'

She obeyed, sitting opposite him, her hair swinging as she kept nodding her head and her voice rose excitedly. When she had finished, he frowned.

'Oh dear, just as I've bullied you into being the perfect secretary! I suppose I must let you go . . . will you postpone it for a week and train one of those idiots in the pool? Last time you were ill, I nearly went mad. The girl I had couldn't even spell, and as for the filing cabinet . . .'

The phone bell shrilled loudly. It was a long-distance call and Cindy waited while he talked. Her thoughts were racing round in circles like a little trapped mouse. A mixture of beautiful lakes, mountains topped with snow, and a castle . . . a real castle . . .

When Patrick Jenkins replaced the receiver he looked at Cindy. He sighed dramatically, but she saw the twinkle in his green eyes.

'When will you grow up?' he asked sadly. 'You've forgotten your glasses again and you walk around, your head stuck forward like an ostrich's, your eyes screwed up.'

Cindy's cheeks burned. 'I know . . . I forgot

14

them because I was so excited.'

'You're always *forgetting* them. A subconscious refusal to wear them, I imagine. Now why?'

'Well . . .' Cindy wriggled about on the seat uncomfortably. Put into words it sounded so stupid. 'My cousins used to tease me a lot. I was called Gobbly-eyed Cindy and they said . . . they said I looked pretty awful in them as I was so ugly in the beginning. I . . . well . . .' Her voice tailed away weakly.

He looked grave. 'What utter tripe! I find you extremely pretty and I think you're even prettier when you're wearing glasses.'

'You do?' Cindy looked so startled Patrick Jenkins found it hard not to laugh.

'I do. Now . . .' he glanced at his watch, 'maybe we'd better get some work done. You can go next week, but come back quickly.' He smiled. 'I shall miss you,' he said so pathetically that they both laughed. 'Now, this Drinkwater firm, for instance. Ready?'

Cindy nodded, pencil poised, as she tried to concentrate on the job in hand.

CHAPTER TWO

The week crawled by for Cindy, impatient as she was to get to the castle that might be hers. She had phoned Mr. Ayres and he had sent her a letter of instructions and had repeated his fears that she would find it too expensive to run *if* the real heir didn't materialise.

Now on the cold wintry day with the sun trying to peep out from behind the clouds, Cindy started on her journey and tried to think of how she *could* find the money required. Whatever happened, she wouldn't sell it. She was used to London traffic and her little grey car slipped in and out until the slow-moving crowded roads of London were left behind and she was on the highways. Here she could settle in the lane she had chosen and let the speed-crazy race by, for she was in no hurry, looking at the countryside with interested eyes. The first part of the journey she found dull, for she loathed flat country. Mountains and lakes and forests, she thought happily, were what she loved. Castle Claife would be so different from this flat uninteresting land. Mr. Ayres had told her the word *Claife* meant *steep hillside with path*, so there must be a special path. Her boss, Mr. Jenkins, had chuckled and said there'd been a lot of smuggling in that part of the world in days gone by—maybe this special path led to a hideaway, as he called it.

Would she ever marry? she wondered. According to her cousins, no man would look twice at her, but Mr. Jenkins had said . . . Suddenly she was laughing happily. He really was a pet, so kind and understanding. Of course he had said that to boost her morale, and it certainly had.

The scenery began to change, the roads to curve, the hills to appear, and she sang gaily as she drove along. She had a feeling that everything was going to be all right.

Then the fog came down without warning. A frightening moment as the cars vanished in the swirling mist. It grew worse and while still in the fast lane cars whizzed by, Cindy crawled along, nose to tail in the long line of cautious drivers as they felt their way. The sight of a motel loomed up through the mist, so Cindy turned off and decided to spend the night there if the fog didn't lift. She tried to phone Claife Castle, but was told the line was out of order. Probably the fog had reached them so Mrs. Stone would understand, she thought as she sat, pretending to read a magazine and finding her thoughts going back again and again to that morning when she had heard from the solicitors and stood in the hall, trying to read the names that she couldn't see—and then that stranger had spoken to her. That was the amazing thing. She didn't know him, but he kept coming into her thoughts. If only she

17

had not forgotten her glasses and had seen him properly. Somehow she couldn't forget him. He seemed to haunt her. Had it been his voice? Deep and—what was the word? Oh yes, *authoritative*, a favourite word used frequently by her boss! It was amazing how easy she had found it to talk to the stranger and—she had to smile—how cross he had made her by teasing her about her age and height, as well as her glasses. Yet he had done it nicely, not rudely.

She walked round the room restlessly. Why must she keep thinking of this man she would never see again? Had she bored him terribly? she wondered. Yet if she had, surely he could easily have ended the conversation and walked away?

The fog was still thick, so she must definitely spend the night there at the motel. She dined early to go to bed and sleep, for she was tired. But whether it was excitement about the castle or fear lest the fog persist for days and so shorten her stay in Claife Castle, for she must remember the real heir might turn up, Cindy didn't know, but she could not sleep that night. Lying awake, tossing and turning, plumping up the pillows, her mind returned time and again to the stranger she could not forget.

Why had he made such an impression on her? she wondered. It was absurd, because she hadn't even seen his face properly nor knew the colour of his eyes.

The fog had gone in the morning. Relieved and with the excitement flooding her veins, she ate a hasty breakfast and then, with Mr. Ayres' painstakingly careful descriptions of how to find the castle by her side, Cindy set off. Now the mountains she loved appeared as the roads wove round the lakes and through the sleepy stone-house villages. It was absurd, she knew, but she felt that she was going *home.* Yet how could it be *home* simply because when she was seven, she had spent a few weeks there?

The beauty seemed to grow the further she drove. The mountains with their golden-brown bracken and the clumps of trees reflected in the quiet stillness of the water seemed to be welcoming her. This was the life she loved, Cindy thought happily. Quietness, serenity . . . that was a good word. She felt serene here, free from troubles, far from the humiliation Oliver had caused her, far from the loneliness of life in big cities, far from the squabbles at the office, the pettiness she hated. Maybe she was what is called a *loner*, Cindy thought as she drove carefully along the twisting roads, enjoying the glimpses of blue water or a quick look at a square-towered church tucked away in a small village.

At last she was getting near Claife Castle. She knew because a large beautiful lake was Windermere. Of course the quiet roads would be very different in the summer months, but then, tucked up in the castle, she needn't see them.

If the castle is yours, she told herself quickly. After all, the real heir might suddenly turn up at any moment.

Ambleside! She recognised the name on the signpost and knew that she could not be far. Slowing up by the side of the road, she read the directions.

'After Ambleside, you'll see a crossroads, take the sharp turn to the left . . . after about ten miles, you'll see a white signpost on the right. This leads to the castle.'

She drove on slowly. Mr. Ayres was right. The crossroads, then further on the white post with the words *Claife Castle* painted on it.

It was only a track with deep corrugations, so she drove slowly up the side of the hill and round it, until she found herself on a plateau. Far below was a lake, a strange-looking one absurdly the shape of a heart. Grassy slopes went down to the water's edge while clumps of trees, their bare branches like animated fingers of a ballet dancer, were silhouetted against the bright sky. Then she saw the entrance to the castle. This she had not remembered, and it took her breath away. An old stone lodge with small windows, while on one side were two castellated towers with heavy wrought-iron gates between them that were closed.

Cindy hooted and a short fat man with a cap

pulled over his eyes, wearing a thick pullover and corduroy breeches and wellingtons, came hobbling out and gave her a quick look.

'I'm Miss Preston,' Cindy called. 'Mrs. Stone is expecting me.'

He came close to the car, his weatherbeaten face sour, his eyes suspicious. 'Has ta been afore?'

'No, this is my first visit,' Cindy told him, and smiled.

He pursed his mouth and nodded slowly. 'I'll be seeing you now,' he told her, and moved off to open the gates.

'Thanks,' Cindy called, but he had turned his back as if glad to see the last of her. She wondered why.

Feeling a little shattered at his unfriendly welcome, she drove on more slowly down a curving narrow drive, hemmed in by tall bushes she thought might be rhododendrons. Down below, through gaps in the bushes she could see a small village, the houses huddled together near the lake, but then as she drove round a corner she had eyes only for what lay ahead.

The castle! It was even more fabulous than she had remembered. She slowed down to look at it—a huge square collection of castellated towers, joined together by grey stone blocks with narrow slits of windows and heavy wooden doors. Further round the building the windows were larger. There was a

21

narrow moat and a drawbridge down.

She just could not believe it. They called it a mock castle! It was exactly the kind of castle you thought of for fairy stories where the princess is rescued by the handsome prince. Beautiful, time-kissed grey stone and far below, the blue of the lake. What more could you want?

A car was parked on the gravel square before the castle, so Cindy parked alongside, took out her suitcase and walked over the drawbridge to the front door. She had to keep turning to look at the lake below or up at the trees that made a pretence of protecting the castle from the winds that must blow fiercely at times.

A huge carved brass lion's head was on the door, so Cindy knocked. Silence. It seemed endless, so she knocked again. The door groaned and squeaked but slowly opened. Cindy caught her breath as she and the woman facing her stared at one another. Cindy found it hard to believe her eyes, wondering if this was some kind of joke, for the woman looked like a tall scarecrow, her grey hair drawn tightly back from her forehead and neck with wisps of hair that had escaped. Her high cheekbones made her face almost like a skull, the skin taut and grey, her mouth drooping at the corners, her chin spotty, and her eyes—! Her eyes were a strange grey and cold with hatred.

'Mrs. Stone,' Cindy said politely, smiling a little nervously. 'I'm Miss Preston.'

'You were to come yesterday,' the shrill impatient voice accused.

'I know, Mrs. Stone, but there was a bad fog and I had to spend the night on the way.'

'You could have let me know.'

'I tried to, but I was told the phone at Claife Castle was out of order.'

Mrs. Stone frowned. 'Is it?' she said accusingly, almost as if it was Cindy's fault. 'I'll get Paul to go down to the village and complain.' She turned away, putting her hands to her mouth and bellowing: 'Paul . . . Paul!'

Cindy fidgeted a little and put down her case, for what else could she do? Short of pushing her way past the housekeeper, she had to wait.

In a moment, a long-legged man in blue jeans and a pullover came running. His fair hair curled on his shoulders, his eyes as he looked at Cindy were angry.

'So she's here now,' he said.

'Paul, the phone isn't working. Go down to the village,' Mrs. Stone told him.

Paul looked Cindy up and down, his eyes narrowed.

'I'll go now.'

He bounded off to the car Cindy had seen parked and with a great roar and strange hooting, went off down the drive. Mrs. Stone looked at Cindy.

'The phone was working in the morning.'

'Well, it wasn't in the late afternoon,' Cindy said, trying not to be annoyed, though Mrs. Stone's voice had almost implied that she was a liar. 'At least that's what the exchange said.'

Mrs. Stone didn't answer and then turned away. 'You'd better come in,' she said reluctantly, almost as if she wished she could think of an alternative.

Cindy followed, carrying her suitcase. In the hall, she paused, looking up at the lofty rafters, the stationary soldiers in armour that stood about, the wide curved staircase.

Mrs. Stone paused on the stairs, looking round. 'Are you coming now?' she said crossly.

'Of course.' Cindy followed the older woman up the uncarpeted stairs, looking round curiously. Everything was old but also very shabby, she noticed, as if no money had been spent on the castle in years. Perhaps it hadn't been, for according to Keith Ayres, Uncle Robert had had financial troubles.

Mrs. Stone opened a door, stood back dramatically to let Cindy in, staring at her as if wondering what Cindy's reaction would be.

Cindy gasped, because it was like going into a museum—a huge four-poster bed with a torn but clean apricot-coloured silk bedspread, a dark brown carpet, heavy dark green curtains hanging either side of a big window. Cindy acted impulsively. Dropping her suitcase, she ran across the room. It was indeed a beautiful

24

view, for they were above the trees and she could see the whole steep slope down to the lake with the gentle mountains on the other side. It was so beautiful.

'The bathroom is down the passage. The door is open,' Mrs. Stone said, but Cindy only heard her as from a long distance. 'Lunch will be served at one o'clock,' then a pause and Mrs. Stone's voice rose so shrilly that Cindy was jerked back to the present and turned round to meet the cold suspicious eyes that glared at her. 'And how long will you be staying now?' Mrs. Stone demanded.

'A week, Mr. Ayres suggested,' Cindy told her, wondering at the animosity she saw.

'Ugh!' Mrs. Stone grunted, turned away and left the room, closing the door with a gentle bang that was far more expressive of her temper than a loud slam might have been.

'But why is she so mad at me?' Cindy wondered as she hastily unpacked. Glancing at her watch, she saw she had an hour to spend before lunch. She decided to stroll around, hoping to keep out of Mrs. Stone's way.

The castle was every bit as fascinating as Cindy had remembered, and yet it was different, not less beautiful or exciting, but sadly shabby as if no one had bothered about it for years. It was clean, the beautiful antique furniture well polished, so Mrs. Stone was not to be blamed. It was as if the owner of the castle had either ceased to care—or had given

25

it up as hopeless, knowing he had not the money needed to revive it. Another favourite expression of Mr. Jenkins', Cindy thought with a smile, wondering how he and Maggie, who was relieving for her, were getting on.

Wandering round the castle, it was difficult for Cindy not to feel some dismay. She now understood what Keith Acres had meant when he talked of money. It would need thousands of pounds to bring the castle back to what it once was. And where could she find thousands of pounds? Perhaps the antiques could be sold and the money raised could be spent on new curtains and carpets, as well as repairs to the cracks in some of the walls.

Coming to an open door, Cindy stepped outside. The crisp cold air stung her cheeks, but she stood still, breathing deeply. There must be a way . . . there had to be. But where was she to find it?

Walking round the garden, she decided that Paul Stone was not the hard worker his mother was, nor as conscientious. Cindy knew little about gardening, but it seemed to her that this garden was in a shocking state. Long tough grass, weeds everywhere, trees and bushes that needed pruning. Surely Uncle Robert must have noticed.

Glancing at her watch, Cindy had to hurry, for she didn't want to give Mrs. Stone more reason for her hostility.

The lunch was delicious, well cooked and

CHAPTER THREE

Somehow Cindy walked along the narrow pavement, her mind in a whirl. Why had he been so rude to her? Maybe he hadn't recognised her in her glasses? Perhaps *he* was short-sighted. She found herself making excuses for his behaviour, yet it all boiled down to one thing and that was what shocked her so. He hadn't wanted to see her again. It was a real brush-off.

She noticed a small tea-shop and went in and sat down. It was empty, but Cindy didn't mind. She wanted to be alone so that she could think. What could she have done to annoy him so? For annoyed he had been. She shivered as she remembered the coldness in his eyes.

Though perhaps his eyes were always cold? After all, she reminded herself, she hadn't seen his eyes before. Yet his voice had been so different. Here, it was so curt.

'Excuse me,' was all he had said.

Yet in London he had teased her, joked and even been sarcastic, but there had been no curt coldness in her voice.

Suddenly a tall girl came from the back of the shop. Cindy gazed in amazement. Why, she was beautiful! A real *model* type, tall, with long slender legs well revealed by the elegance of her sea-green skirt and pale cream tunic.

She had high cheekbones and surprisingly dark eyes as compared with her blonde hair which was beautifully curled.

'I'm sorry I didn't hear you come in,' the girl said. 'Would you like some tea?'

'Please,' said Cindy.

When the tea came, the tall girl smiled. 'Mind if I join you? One gets so bored here with never a new face. You're Miss Preston, now?'

Cindy looked startled. 'Yes, how did you know?'

The girl laughed. 'Everything is known in the village. The castle will be yours if Peter Baxter doesn't turn up. Right?'

'Yes, but . . .'

'He still may, though I doubt it. I'm Johanna Younge.' She smiled ruefully. 'Believe it or not, I was once a beauty queen, then, like an idiot, I fell in love with a country boy and here I am.' She waved her hand vaguely. 'Thirty-five and stuck in this dump—a widow looking for a rich husband. Thought I'd found one, but it seems he's not as wealthy as I thought.' She laughed. 'Nor as interested.'

Cindy stirred her tea slowly. 'Why stay here?' she asked.

Johanna shrugged. 'Because I'm a fool. I love him.'

'Oh,' said Cindy. She couldn't think of anything else to say. What *did* one say? A startling frightening thought struck her. Was *she* in love? In love with a man she'd only met once—no, twice if you could count today's a *meeting*? If not, why was she so upset? If he was just an ordinary man, would she care?

'This place does well in the summer, but in the winter . . . well, you can see for yourself. Every year I swear that next year I'll go to London, but I stay here. I know I'm a fool.'

In the distance the telephone bell shrilled. Johanna Younge quickly drank her tea and stood up. She smiled at Cindy.

'The village is coming to life, I think. You're the second southerner we've had here in the last week. Both interested in the castle, too. The castle! What a farce—it's no more a castle than I'm a beauty!' Johanna shrugged as she walked away.

Cindy drank her tea slowly and ate the delicious scones with jam and cream. She glanced at her watch. The sun was still shining —should she drive around or . . .

Johanna joined her again. 'Sorry about that. Wrong number as usual. Look, if you want to know anything about the castle—and you'd be very odd if you didn't—I suggest you go along and see old Mrs. Usher. She's lived here all her life. Never been outside the village and, hard as it is to believe, never wants to go anywhere else. She'll tell you about the castle and the Baxters.' Her voice was bitter.

'You don't like them?'

Johanna shrugged. 'I met Peter once or

twice and liked him, but of course David, his cousin, and he never hit it off. I don't know why. The old man I never knew—bit of a recluse, you see. Didn't like visitors—at least, according to his housekeeper.' Johanna chuckled. 'Now there's a broken heart for you!'

'Mrs. Stone?' Cindy was startled.

The phone bell shrilled again. Cindy stood up, hastily paid for her tea and left.

Outside she looked up and down. There was not a soul in sight. Somehow she didn't feel in the mood for driving round and she had an absurd urge to learn more about the castle. What was the old lady's name? Usher! That was it!

Cindy went into the Post Office, chose two postcards with lovely pictures of Windermere, wrote quickly on each to say she was fine, and then got stamps. The postmistress, fat and cheerful, beamed.

'Did Mr. Baxter knock you down?' she asked.

'Mr. Baxter?' Cindy echoed, puzzled. Mr. Baxter was dead, she nearly said.

'I saw it happen. You were coming into the shop now and out he went, storming like a madman because the telegram he's expecting hasn't arrived. Not my fault, and I told him so—'

'Was that Mr. Baxter who bumped into me?' Cindy blinked her eyes, shaking her head, for

34

her mind felt muzzy. 'But . . .'

'Yes, David Baxter, the late Robert Baxter's nephew.' The postmistress chuckled. 'I bet he's feeling mad. Did you have a cup of tea? I guessed that was where you were now. What do you think of our local beauty queen?' she chuckled again.

'I thought she was very beautiful.'

'So she is—but he just doesn't see her.'

'He?' Cindy said, puzzled.

'David—David Baxter. Johanna is crazy about him, seems like he prefers to be a bachelor.'

Cindy drew a long deep breath.

'Mrs. Younge is in love with David Baxter?' Cindy said slowly. Gone was her last hope. How could a short ugly girl who wore glasses compete with such a beauty?

The postmistress gave her the stamps with another chuckle.

'We all thought once they were going to wed, and then he changed. It's ever since his uncle died that he's been so bitter. Not that I'm surprised, mind.' Her eyes narrowed. 'Are you Miss Preston?' she asked, her voice losing its friendliness suddenly.

Cindy felt uncomfortable. Now what had she said to upset the postmistress? Why had her attitude changed so suddenly? At that moment, the door bell clanged and two elderly women came in chatting. Both stopped talking as they saw Cindy and she hurried past them, uncomfortably aware that they were staring at her.

In the street, she hesitated, looking up and down, An elderly man in breeches and a jacket, his cap pulled over one eye, paused.

'Where's ta gaan?' he asked sympathetically.

Cindy smiled. 'I'm looking for Mrs. Usher.'

'She'll be there any time. Fourth cottage on the left—a dog in t'garden. He don't bite now.' He smiled, touched his cap and hobbled by her.

Hurrying down the street, Cindy found the cottage. A typical Lake District cottage, she was to learn in the days ahead, with a door and four windows. A beautifully cared-for garden with snowdrops in flower and some of the bushes showing green buds. A spaniel lying on the white doorstep stood up and wagged his tail friendly.

The door opened instantly, and a tiny woman stood in the doorway. A thin woman whose dark grey woollen frock hung loosely on her narrow shoulders. Her skin was perfect, rosy pink as though the crisp air acted as a tonic. Her eyes shone.

'Miss Preston,' she said with a warm welcoming smile. 'I hoped you'd come and see me.'

'I ... it ...' Cindy began. 'The village knows everything.'

'But of course, and you are news. Do come in. I hope you aren't allergic to cats, dogs or budgies, because I've got the lot!' She opened the door wider and Cindy walked in.

The main room was surprisingly big with a huge log fire crackling merrily and a tray of tea and cakes waiting. As Cindy went in several cats stood up, stretched, took one look at her and lay down again. Two dogs came racing, one a gracefully slender greyhound, the other a Corgi who gave Cindy a good look up and down, then turned away and lay down. Pushed gently into a deep comfortable armchair, Cindy was given a cup of tea and induced to eat some of the delicious home-made cakes.

Mrs. Usher never stopped talking. She had an attractive voice with a sort of Welsh lilt. 'I'm so glad you've come, dear, I hoped you'd be here earlier, but I suppose it was the fog, because we expected you yesterday—and how do you like the castle? Rather sad, isn't it, poor Robert was a generous man and the castle suffered for it.'

She poured out another cup of tea and then sat back in her chair, folded her hands and smiled at Cindy. 'Now what do you want to know, dear?'

Cindy didn't know what to say. After all, what did she want to know? She grabbed at the first thing that came into her mind.

'Why is David Baxter so bitter? The postmistress told me how he'd changed after his uncle died and . . . and I met Mrs. Younge and she said he had changed—and what I can't

37

understand is that I met him by chance in London and . . . we talked. You see, it was like this . . .' Cindy told the white-haired old lady the whole story. 'He was so different in London. Not rude and . . . cold as he was here,' Cindy finished.

'I didn't know he'd been to London lately,' Mrs. Usher said thoughtfully, 'but you travel so fast these days that you're often back before you know you're going.'

They laughed together.

'He is bitter, but it's natural like. You see . . . you see, he always thought he'd be his uncle's heir.'

'Oh, he thought he'd get Claife Castle?' Cindy frowned. 'But why didn't he tell me when I told him about the castle? He must have known it would be the same one.'

Mrs Usher shrugged. 'The Baxters have always been a funny lot. I've known them all my life.'

Driving home to the castle an hour later, Cindy thought of all Mrs. Usher had told her: how Robert Baxter had been a domineering man and his wife very quiet and biddable. Peter had been like his father, yet different—where his father knew he was always right, Peter Baxter queried it and was willing to accept advice. The one thing he had been adamant about, though, had been his refusal to go into his father's business. Peter wanted to be an engineer. So they had quarrelled.

38

'Very sad indeed,' Mrs. Usher had said. 'I think poor Robert often regretted his own obstinacy and probably poor Peter wished they could have seen eye to eye. Peter was a nice lad. I was fond of him and sorry, too. He hated hurting anyone, but sometimes you have to. Then David took over the job that should have been Peter's. When Robert grew older and was suffering from gout, he sold his business to David at a very reasonable, almost absurd figure. A generous man, Robert, but sometimes foolish. David was certain he would inherit the castle and everything. When he heard about you . . . an unknown stranger . . .'

And yet, Cindy thought as she drove carefully up towards the castle, David had shown no anger or coldness in London and he must have known she was the girl who had literally stolen the castle from him, though without knowing it.

One thing, she told herself, this settled her stupid dream about him. No wonder he didn't want to know her!

She drove the car round behind the castle and parked it in one of the open garages. Paul was in the yard, but he ignored her. Cindy was tempted to go to him and say how sorry she was—yet could she say that truthfully? she wondered. Mrs. Usher had explained Mrs. Stone's animosity.

'She hoped that Robert would leave Paul the castle. Why she should think that I don't know. After all, they'd only been with him ten years. Again Robert was too generous. He paid for a good education for Paul, but look what the boy's like now—a typical hippy, lazy as they come. Adored by his mother, of course, who sees no fault in him.'

Cindy had sighed. 'It makes me feel pretty miserable. I didn't want to hurt all these people.'

Mrs. Usher had smiled. 'Not to worry, dear child. Robert often talked to me of you. He loved your mother, you see. That's why you were asked to stay here. Unfortunately your mother said no and that was that, but he never forgot how you loved the castle. He knew, you see, that both the Stones and David would sell the castle. Only Peter wouldn't . . . nor you.'

Now as Cindy hurried to her bedroom to change into another frock, she wondered just *how* she was going to keep the castle going— always of course allowing for the fact that Peter didn't turn up. How David must hate her, she thought unhappily. Why, oh, why had she to meet a man she liked so much on sight only to find he hated her?

CHAPTER FOUR

Cindy was very quiet as Mrs. Stone served up dinner. Cindy had never felt so uncomfortable before in her life. She had no desire to hurt the Stones or David Baxter; indeed, she herself had nothing to do with it—but perhaps they didn't realise that? What was there she could say? Unable to answer that question, Cindy decided it might be wiser to keep quiet.

Afterwards she sat alone in the huge cold drawing-room before a log fire that crackled and sparkled. How quiet everything was. If she ever lived there, Cindy decided, she would certainly have a dog, or even several, and some cats. How wonderful to have a real home—not just a box-like bed-sitter where you had to ease your way round the furniture that took up what little space there was. Suddenly restless, she got up and wandered down the lofty dark hall, dimly lit by a very old chandelier that looked as if it might fall at any moment.

The click-clack of her heels on the polished floor sounded absurdly loud and echoed and re-echoed as she went from room to room. There was little difference in them, for they were all full of old antiques—each article amazingly clean and polished. Mrs. Stone certainly worked hard, Cindy thought. Poor Mrs. Stone—her dream demolished.

41

The library was the most interesting, even though it was so cold. Cindy walked past the crowded bookshelves, looking for something to read.

After she had collected several books that looked interesting—all biographies—she paused by the huge old desk, and opened it. There were a few papers in it, neatly folded, so obviously whoever had gone through Uncle Robert's papers had taken everything of value. It was a fascinating desk with so many drawers and shelves of different size. She had a job getting one drawer shut, and as she pushed and pulled it, a small door-like board swung open.

'A secret drawer!' she said slowly, her eyes wide with excitement. Of course many of these old desks had secret drawers, she knew. She put in her hand and slowly pulled out a long thin flat book. Opening it, she peered at the incredibly tiny neat writing. It was hard to read.

Suddenly she heard footsteps—angry ones, she thought, as they went clomp, clomp, clomp, along. It could only be Mrs. Stone!

Hastily Cindy closed the desk, pushed the flat book under her cardigan and moved to the bookshelves.

'What do you think you're doing now?' Mrs. Stone demanded. Standing in the doorway, her hands on hips, cheeks flushed, hair more wispy than usual, her eyes were angry.

'I was getting something to read,' Cindy explained, gathering the books up.

'You've not the right to meddle about with Mr. Baxter's things,' Mrs. Stone said angrily. 'The castle ain't yours yet, nor may it ever be if Mr. Baxter turns up.'

'I'm sure Mr. Baxter wouldn't object to my reading some of his many books,' Cindy said, lifting her head and returning, glare by glare, Mrs. Stone's angry looks. 'I was thinking how wonderfully clean you've kept the castle,' she added.

Mrs. Stone sniffed. 'Someone has to, haven't they? Not easy, mind, nor appreciated. Mr. Baxter never saw if it was clean or t'dirt was around.'

Somehow Cindy managed to escape and went back to sit by her fire. She looked through the books, keeping the long flat book under a cushion. She wondered why she had hidden it so quickly—after all, whoever went through Mr. Baxter's things must have known of the secret drawer. Yet something had told her to keep it from Mrs. Stone. Cindy realised with a shock that not only did she dislike Mrs. Stone but she distrusted her—and disliked and distrusted the son, Paul, even more.

The quietness was so oppressively still—the only sound being the occasional crackle of a twig fallen off the log as it was burned through—that Cindy found herself looking

43

constantly over her shoulder. In the end she went to bed, propped up by pillows, and began to read the long flat book she had found.

It was very hard to read the tiny neat writing! Cindy tried both with and without her glasses. She read enough to realise it was Robert Baxter's diary. Not a very, very old one as she had hoped, perhaps dating back to the eighteenth century would have been much more exciting.

Yet in a way she wanted to know more about the man who had never forgotten her, who had remembered how, as a little girl of seven, she had wept because her mother said the castle wasn't *real* . . . As Cindy read, she realised it was not a diary, but more a collection of notes he had made.

'Sometimes I feel I cannot survive unless I have someone to talk to. This is why I am writing this,' Cindy read. 'The quiet emptiness is the most devastating experience I have ever known. If only Peter would write! Just a few words, so that I know he is well. How can I write to him when I have no idea where he is?'

Cindy closed the book with a sigh. As Mrs. Usher had said, how terribly sad. Yet surely Peter Baxter *could* have written to his father? Or was the quarrel too bitter to allow a proud man to make the first move?

At breakfast next day, Mrs. Stone told Cindy that Mr. Fairhead wished to speak to her.

44

'He manages the estate,' Mrs. Stone explained. 'A mean man if ever there was one.'

Cindy wondered what sort of man he was that she went out to meet. He was standing in front of the castle, frowning as he looked down at the lake below. As she joined him she saw she hadn't realised just how high up the castle stood, but now she could see the winding narrow track and two cars were going along it that looked like toy cars scuttling along.

The man turned to look at her, his eyes narrowed thoughtfully. He was a big burly man with a slight tummy bulge and grey tufty hair. He held out his hand.

'I felt I'd like t'know you, Miss Preston. Seems like you may be my boss.' His grin split his weatherbeaten face in half. He shook her hand firmly and frowned. 'You're younger than I expected.'

Cindy's chin tilted. 'I'm nearly twenty.'

He grinned. 'You remind me of my daughter. She's nearly sixteen.' Luke Fairhead had a dog beside him. 'This is Bessie, a farmer's best friend.'

The sheepdog looked up as Cindy stroked her ears.

'You're lucky,' Luke Fairhead said. 'The sun isn't always with us.'

'I don't mind if it rains, Mr. Fairhead. I think this is so lovely.'

He beamed again. 'You like it here?'

'So much. I never forgot it, you know.'

'It's gone to seed badly. You . . .' Mr. Fairhead looked embarrassed. 'We know nought about you, Miss Preston. If you do inherit the castle, will you be able to . . .'

'Finance it?' Cindy looked at him. 'I don't know. There must be some way. Other beautiful old places manage.'

'But, Miss Preston, Claife Castle is different. It isn't really *old*.'

'I know. Mr. Ayres, the solicitor, told me so. Yet there must be a way.'

'I'd like you to come to my office and then let me show you around, Miss Preston. I think it's only fair for you to see the bad side as well as the good of your inheritance.'

'But Mr. Fairhead . . .' Cindy put out her hand and touched his arm, 'I think you're forgetting that I'm not the *heiress* to the castle. There's still time for the son to turn up.'

'No, Miss Preston, that I haven't forgotten. Peter was a strange lad with a habit of turning up unexpectedly. Real sad, that quarrel with his dad. The old man was always sure he was right and Peter had the same kink, but different-like, if you know what I mean. I'll never forget the day he came back—Peter, I mean. It was some years after he'd walked out and I saw the lad arrive. He knocked on the door and spoke to Mrs. Stone. She closed the door in his face and kept him waiting—then when she came back, she told him something and then slammed the door. I never seen Peter

46

look like that. White as a sheep turning sick, that was what he looked like, as if his face had been slapped. He didn't see me . . . he just drove off like a madman.'

'I wonder what she said.'

Mr. Fairhead shrugged. 'I can only guess that the old man refused to see him.'

'But he wanted . . .' Cindy began, and stopped, for the front door behind had opened with its usual squeaks and groans. Mrs. Stone stood there.

'Paul'd like to see you now, Mr. Fairhead.'

Luke Fairhead frowned. 'Tell him I'm busy. I'll see him later. Come on, Miss Preston,' he said, and strode away, Cindy following, trying to keep up with his long strides, straightening the glasses that were sliding down her nose.

It didn't make sense somehow, she was thinking as she hurried. Peter coming to see his father—then the old man refusing to see him? Yet in the notebook she was reading . . .

'Ah, come inside, Miss Preston.' Mr. Fairhead led the way into an immaculately neat office. 'Let's get down to business.'

Two hours later he shook Cindy warmly by the hand. 'Well, you now see the position, Miss Preston. I'm glad you feel as you do. Maybe if we sold the farm—your uncle would not hear of it, but then he didn't realise that he was running it at a loss. Colin Pritchard is too old to manage it really, but Mr. Baxter won't turn him out. A kind man, Mr. Baxter, for all

47

his tempers. His nephew David takes after him for the last. Now there's a bitter young man what's had too much done for him. His uncle was generous.'

'I understand Mr. David Baxter expected to inherit the castle,' Cindy said.

Mr. Fairhead grunted. 'David may have thought it, but not me. Robert Baxter always meant Peter to have it. David would sell the lot tomorrow, and that was something Robert Baxter didn't want.'

'Well . . . well, if I do get it,' Cindy said awkwardly, 'I'll do my best to keep it.'

'I know you will, Miss Preston, and you can count on me for help. Now where's that young layabout, Paul? Round the back, I've no doubt. Another sign of Robert's generosity that goes wrong. Young Stone has been given everything and what does he do in return?—nothing. 'Bye for now.'

He strode off round the castle, Bessie following him. Cindy knocked on the door. She was startled when after the usual squeaking and groaning Paul Stone opened it.

He held out an envelope. 'Letter for you, Miss Preston.' He looked down at it, turning it over. 'Funny thing—it's got a London postmark, but the address on the back is American.'

'So?' Cindy took it, looking down at the address. 'This isn't for me,' she said. 'It's addressed to the owner of Claife Castle. I'm

48

not . . .'

'Yet!' Paul Stone's mouth curled. 'But you will be—eh? Open it and see what it says.' He leaned against the door, making it impossible for her to go into the hall.

'I've got no right to open it. I'm not the owner,' she repeated.

'Don't be square, Miss Preston,' Paul Stone laughed scornfully. 'I bet you're longing to open it just as much as me. What can an American have to do with Claife Castle?'

Cindy shook her head. 'I have no right to open it. I shall send it at once to the solicitor. Please let me pass.'

He shrugged, standing back. 'Okay, if you feel stuffy. I'm going down to the village. Want me to bring you up a newspaper?'

'No, thanks—I'm going down myself.' Cindy told him. 'By the way, Mr. Fairhead is looking for you.'

'Let him look,' Paul said with a grin. 'He made me wait, now it's my turn.' He strode over the gravel towards his bright red car.

Cindy hurried to her bedroom, found an envelope and hastily wrote to Mr. Ayres.

'I've no right to open it, so think it best to send it to you.'

Quickly she put on her thick coat, tied a green scarf round her head and looked in the mirror. She had thick dark rims to her glasses. Did they seem to hide her face? she wondered. Mr. Jenkins had said they made her look

49

prettier, but then he was only being kind. Perhaps she'd meet David Baxter in the village and he might be in a better mood.

CHAPTER FIVE

Cindy drove down to the village by the lake, parked her car and hurried to the Post Office. It had struck her that the letter might be about the missing heir—whoever it was might not know that Robert Baxter was dead but merely that the heir was being sought. As she opened the shop door and entered, the babble of voices stopped with an abruptness that startled her.

How crowded the small shop seemed, for that was what it really was; a stationer's, newsagent and sweet shop with a side made over to be a sub-post office. Now it seemed full of women talking again as they turned their backs on her and she made her way to the post office counter.

She caught words here and there; words spoken loudly as if the speaker hoped they'd be overheard.

'No right t'it, has she?'

'Jumping the bridge afore it's built . . .'

'Of course she musta seen the paper now . . .'

Trying to ignore the crowd, Cindy bought a stamp. The postmistress looked at her with cold eyes.

'Reckon you're pleased with yourself, Miss Preston,' she said. 'A good day to you now.'

Puzzled, Cindy hesitated. What had she to

51

be pleased about? The talk with Mr. Fairhead had been depressing and even alarming, for she could see no solution to the problems she'd have to face if the castle was hers. How could it be a good day? Perhaps she meant the weather?

So Cindy smiled. 'Yes, it is a lovely day, isn't it?'

There was another silence and she felt a cold wave of anger go through the small shop. She hurried outside as fast as she could, almost forgetting to stick the stamp on the envelope and drop it into the letterbox.

Once outside she almost ran to her car. She had to get away. Somehow or other she had angered the villagers. But how? Or why? Maybe it was absurd, she thought unhappily, but it frightened her. It was like walking on the edge of a volcano here—she was never sure when or how she might anger the local people.

As she started the car, she remembered a holiday she had once spent in Cornwall. There an old inhabitant had laughed.

'Take no notice of them,' she had said. 'I've lived here fifty year and I'm still a "furriner". You have to be born here to be accepted.'

Maybe it was the same in the Lake District, Cindy thought as she drove down a road she had never been along. Soon she was driving along a wider road, not sure where she was going, not really caring. Passing a public callbox in a small village, she stopped and put a call through to the castle. Mrs. Stone answered it.

'Oh, it's you now, is it?' she said, her voice impatient. 'Has ta something to tell me?'

Cindy stifled a sigh. 'Just that I shall be out to lunch, Mrs. Stone.'

'Is that so now? I'm not surprised. Celebrating with champagne, I don't doubt!' she said, and slammed down the receiver.

Putting down the receiver too, but slowly, Cindy went out into the cold crisp mountain air. So Mrs. Stone was also mad! What on earth was wrong with them all?

Back in her car, Cindy started to drive. She had no idea where to go, but probably she would find herself in a town at lunch time and could eat there. She felt she could not face Mrs. Stone's cold anger or Paul's cheekiness.

The road lay along the side of the hill, going slowly downwards. One side was covered with heather, the other with huge boulders perilously balanced—or so they looked, while clumps of trees kept hiding the lake that was, as could be expected here, in the valley below. Here it was peaceful, she thought, as she drove through a tiny village. The church was outside, alone in dignified solitude. Nearer the village a house that had to be the vicarage and a church school—then just a row of small shops and a few cottages huddled together as if whispering secrets.

Turning a corner, she found herself

suddenly on a level with the lake. She saw it was a waiting place for a ferry and already two cars were parked, waiting as the flat-bottomed ferry slowly made its way towards them across the sun-sparkled lake. She might as well go across, she thought, and parked behind the cars.

Looking up at the sky, she saw the sun was about to be temporarily hidden by a strangely grey cloud and that behind it darker grey clouds looked ominous. Perhaps the sunny period was over and the rain near? Well, it matched her mood, she thought unhappily, for suddenly everything seemed to have gone wrong and the excited happiness that had filled her ever since she had received Keith Ayres' letter had vanished.

The lake water rippled gently as the ferry came towards them with a strange, slow dignity, almost as if the journey was effortless. On the opposite bank was a large white house down near the water. In the middle of the lake, a small island. If there was a cottage on it, it was hidden by the dense cluster of trees.

Cindy drove on the ferry with the other cars. It was only when she chanced to turn her head she saw that in the car next to hers, David Baxter sat!

Had he seen her? she wondered. He was sitting, his arms folded, his head turned to look the opposite way. Was it on purpose? she asked herself. Then he turned suddenly and

54

caught her staring at him. She half-smiled nervously, but feeling perhaps she should make the first move, and he lifted a newspaper that lay by his side and waved it angrily.

For a moment she thought he was going to throw it at her and then he dropped it down on the seat and deliberately turned his back on her.

She turned away, too, shocked and bewildered. Now what on earth could she have done to have so offended everyone? She stared without really seeing them at the masses of gulls who were swooping down to dive into the water. Suddenly she saw that the white house had become a great deal bigger than before and she realised that the ferry was nearing the opposite shore. Several swans swam slowly past, looking at the ferry arrogantly, almost as if defying it to run them down, Cindy thought, as she tried to forget the look of anger on David Baxter's face as he waved the newspaper at her.

She drove ashore and straight up the hill, concentrating on looking at the scenery to distract her thoughts. She saw a squat little church with a square tower that stood in a churchyard and seemed guarded by a row of dark dignified cypresses that appeared determined to shut out the world. Suddenly she was on a straight road, running alongside the lake but much higher. The grey clouds had moved and the sun shone. How yellow the fields looked, but she knew it was only golden bracken. Up here on the other side of the road she saw the flag walls that Mr. Fairhead had told her about. In the quiet fields sheep were grazing while a few small lambs were gambolling about, having what looked like a lot of fun.

As she drove on, she reached Ambleside. Startled, because she had thought herself much farther from the castle, Cindy stopped and had lunch. She also bought a booklet of coloured pictures of the different parts of the Lake District and decided to drive up past Langdale and towards Keswick. She had no desire to go back to the castle, though she knew she would have to—no matter how long she postponed it.

Now, as she drove, she found herself in a totally different countryside. The mountains seemed larger and they were no longer covered with trees and grass. Bracken, yes, but mostly they were bare rocks. Suddenly it was eerie—the huge grey and green mountains standing high above the quiet lakes threateningly while the distant view was of mountains going away in their curving beauty. She shivered, for now the sun had vanished again and the grey coldness seeped through her warm coat. Realising how late it was, she turned to drive home. Maybe things would be better next day, she thought. She had liked Luke Fairhead; perhaps she could ask him what she had done to offend the local villagers and then she might be able to put the matter right.

Turning a corner, she slowed up instinctively, driving off the road on to the grass verge to stare at the scene before her. It was horribly desolate, yet had a beauty she had never seen before. The mountains had grown dark as the sun fell. Now they were silhouetted against a sky of weird loveliness, a sky of pale grey with streaks of palest mauve and a wonderful clear yellow of the remains of the sunshine—all this reflected in the still lake. Down by the water, stood some trees, their bare branches spread upwards as if appealing to the darkening sky—their delicate twigs looking like fine crochet against the light.

She sighed. How she loved this beauty—if only she could find a way to keep the castle—if, that is, the castle was going to be hers.

It was dark when she reached Claife Castle. She saw a car parked outside, but drove on round the back to the garages. She walked round to the front of the castle, thinking again that there must be a way to find the money to rejuvenate it. Would a bank manager consider her old enough—or reliable enough—to be loaned the money? If she ran it as a hotel . . .

She knocked on the front door. It opened immediately as if Mrs. Stone had been waiting for her. Now she stood back, her face bright with triumph.

'You're late, Miss Preston. I thought you might be lost now. There's a gentleman waiting to see you.'

'A gentleman?' Cindy was startled. Who did she know who'd be visiting her? A sudden rush of hope filled her. Could it be David Baxter? Come to apologise for his strange and rude behaviour?

She pulled off her coat and scarf, running her hands through her hair, and went to the big drawing-room.

A tall man stood by the fire. Now he turned to look at her. It was David Baxter! In his hand was a newspaper.

CHAPTER SIX

He came towards her with no smile or sign of friendliness on his face.

He lifted the newspaper. 'How do you explain this?' he asked.

She stared at him, startled, indeed bewildered. He had changed! His voice was much deeper—his face more suntanned, his fair hair shorter. How could he have changed in so short a time?

'You *are* Mr. Baxter?' she said uncertainly.

'Of course I am. Why else should I be here? I want an explanation of this.' He lifted the paper again as he spoke curtly.

Something seemed to snap inside her. 'About what? I haven't seen a paper today, but I'm absolutely sick of your rudeness. Waving the paper at me on the ferry like that!'

'What on earth are you talking about? What ferry? I drove up from London as soon as I read the article.' Suddenly she knew! It was the voice she had been unable to forget. The voice he had used in London as he teased her about her eyes and her height.

'You *are* . . .' she hesitated. 'You are David Baxter?'

He frowned, his thick eyebrows almost meeting.

'David Baxter? Of course I'm not. I'm Peter

Baxter.'

'Peter!' Without thinking, Cindy put out her hand vaguely and the next moment the man had her by the arms and was gently pushing her into an armchair.

'Let's get this straight,' he said briskly. 'You seem to have had a shock. What made you think I was David Baxter? Incidentally, he's my cousin.'

'I can see now you're so different. I thought when I saw him—that it was you.'

'If you remember, you'd left your glasses behind, so you didn't really know what I looked like.'

'No, I didn't. He was big and tall and fair and . . .' Cindy shook her head slowly, her long hair swinging. 'I'm beginning to understand.'

'Understand what?'

'His behaviour. I spoke to him and he . . .'

'Was rude? He's not noted for his good manners. Has a foul temper, too. What's all this about waving a paper at you?'

'I . . . I was on the ferry . . . I wanted to get away. They were all so unfriendly, I couldn't understand it . . . and then I turned my head and he was in the next car and he looked furious. I thought he was going to throw the paper at me and . . .'

'I see.' Peter pulled up a small straight-backed chair and straddled it, looking at her thoughtfully. 'You haven't read the paper today?' He passed it to her. 'I suggest you read the front page article. It might explain a lot of things.'

Cindy opened the paper and stared at the headlines.

TEENAGER PLANS TO SELL MOCK CASTLE SHE MAY INHERIT FOR TWENTY THOUSAND POUNDS

Underneath it said: 'A nineteen-year-old girl who may become heiress to a mock castle in Cumberland has been offered twenty thousand pounds by an American who plans to demolish the castle and rebuild it, stone by stone, in America. A distant ancestor of his lived in the castle soon after it was built and he has always wanted to live in it himself—but in his own country. Of course there is always the possibility that the real heir—the son of the deceased—may appear. No one seems to know why this girl, who is no relation to the Baxter family, should have been made heiress at all. She said that if the castle is hers, she will sell it to the American. Local people are angrily against the project. It is their castle, they say, not hers.'

Cindy looked up as she finished reading. 'But it isn't!' she said, her voice shocked. 'No American has offered me twenty thousand pounds.' Her hand flew to her mouth. 'Today, just before lunch, there was a letter for me. But it wasn't really for *me*—it was addressed to the owner . . . so I sent it to Mr. Ayres . . .'

'After opening it?'

Cindy frowned. 'I didn't open it. I am . . . was not the owner, so I went straight down to the village and posted it off.'

'Paul Stone says you opened it and smiled.'

Cindy was on her feet. 'Paul is lying.' She glared at the man. 'Of course, if you prefer to believe him . . .' She turned and walked to the door, but Peter Baxter was quickly on his feet, grabbing her by the arms, turning her round.

'Where do you think you're going?'

'To pack my clothes and drive back to London. I have no right to be here now.'

'I agree.' Surprisingly, he smiled. 'All the same, I'm not allowing a slip of a girl like you to drive back to London alone in the dark. You stay here tonight,' he said quietly—very quietly, so quietly that she looked at him quickly. It had been an order, not a suggestion.

'Why should I?'

He smiled. 'Because I say so, and I'm a lot stronger than you.' He bent one arm, pretending to flex his muscles.

She found herself laughing. 'Are you threatening me?'

'Not really. Now I'll ask you politely: Please stay the night. It's going to be foggy and Keith Ayres would never forgive me if anything happened to you.'

'Keith Ayres?' she was puzzled. 'You mean the solicitor?'

'Who else?' Peter Baxter chuckled. 'Don't tell me you didn't notice? He fell for you, hook, line and sinker.' He laughed. 'He thinks you're . . . well, quite something.'

'But I only met him once!' Cindy was startled. 'I liked him, but . . .'

'There was no "but" about his liking for you. Although he was pleased to see me, he was equally disappointed because you wanted the castle and he knew I didn't.'

'You don't!' Cindy took a step backwards and his hand fell off her arm.

'No, I've always hated it, but . . .' He led her back to the chair. 'Sit down and let's talk about this sanely.'

She sat down. 'Look, Mr. Baxter . . .'

'Please call me Peter, and you're . . . ?'

'Cindy—Lucinda Preston.' She leaned forward. 'Mr . . . I mean Peter, I just don't understand. You met me in London, I told you all about the castle and the missing son. You must have known it was Claife Castle.'

'Of course I did. I'd seen the advertisement and wasn't very keen to claim the heritage. I knew it would probably cost me more than it was worth. My memories of this place are not particularly happy, but I was persuaded that it was my duty.' He smiled ruefully. 'An example of the power of a woman being underestimated. In a way, she was right. I went there, met you and realised how much the castle meant to you, so I decided not to make a claim but to let you have it.'

'You were going to let me have it?' Cindy stared at him in amazement. 'But it's yours!'

'Then let's see it as a gift to you. At least . . .' his voice suddenly changed, 'it *was* to be a gift. I didn't realise the first thing you'd do would be to sell it. Seeing that my father left it to you because he believed you loved it . . . well, it made me change my mind about you.'

'But I knew nothing about the sale. How could I sell something that wasn't mine?' Cindy twisted her hair round one hand. 'Look,' she leaned forward, 'I only got that letter before lunch. This article was in the morning's paper. I knew nothing about it.'

'That, of course, would be your story,' he said. Again his voice was cold and unfriendly. 'The letter today might have been an acknowledgement of your acceptance of the offer.'

She let go of her hair, shook her head and leaned back.

'You think I'm that sort of person?'

'No, I didn't think so. I don't. All the same, I gathered from Keith Ayres that you have no money of your own, only the pittance you earn—' He smiled suddenly. 'I gather you're a careful saver and have your own car, but as he said, that's hardly enough to run a castle this size. I know he arranged for you to see Luke as well. I'm sure he depressed and frightened you about the money needed. It is a heavy burden

64

to put on a teenager's shoulders. In fact, my father should have known better. Of course Ayres wanted you to sell it.'

'But why?' Cindy was bewildered. Keith Ayres had seemed so nice.

Peter Baxter chuckled. 'Because he wants you in London, of course.' He stood up. 'Look, I fancy a drink, and I expect you can do with one. I suggest you go and have a quick wash and change into a pretty frock and then we'll have a drink and something to eat. We might as well enjoy this evening.'

She stood up. 'Enjoy?' she said slowly. 'Enjoy?'

Peter turned and looked at her. 'Please don't do anything dramatic and run away. My car is faster than yours, so I would soon catch you. Besides, the fog has come down pretty badly. See you in ten minutes,' he said, and left the room.

She moved very slowly. Her limbs felt heavy and tired. Somehow she walked upstairs and into her ice-cold bedroom. Rather like a robot she moved, washing, finding her pale green trouser suit and changing, brushing her hair and pinning it up on her head, she looked anxiously in the mirror. Should she wear her glasses or not? she asked herself. She decided she had better wear them or else it would give him an opportunity to tease her. What a funny face she had! Her cousins were right. What man in his senses would look twice at her?

Peter's jokes about the solicitor liking her just proved it. He—Peter, that was—was only being kind—just as Mr. Jenkins had been. How small her face was—with the strange oval look and the big round glasses. She pulled them off, but then her reflection was blurred. Maybe that was why she thought she was better-looking without them, she told herself, and put the glasses on again.

She looked round her. Her last night in what she had thought was—or might be—her own castle. She went to the window. The fog was thick, curling itself round in the darkness like the cloak of a witch who was flying by on her broomstick.

The long flat book she had found in the secret drawer was safely locked in her suitcase. She would read it that night, she decided, and then give it to Peter. It was his by rights, yet she wanted badly to read it, for there were several things that puzzled her.

For one thing, Mrs. Stone saying that Peter had never come to see his father, yet Luke Fairhead had said he had *seen* Peter come, and also seen him turned away *by* Mrs. Stone, 'his face white as a sheep being sick'. Cindy would have trusted Luke Fairhead any day before Mrs. Stone. And why had Paul Stone lied about the letter? He had been the one who wanted her to open it. He must have lied deliberately, but why? What for?

In addition, there were the nice things Mrs.

Usher had said about Peter Baxter. And she knew him well. As Mrs. Stone implied, if Peter so hated his father, would he deliberately shoulder what he had called the 'burden' of the castle simply because he had believed Cindy was prepared to sell it, which was something his father would have hated?

It didn't make sense. There were too many contradictions. Perhaps reading Uncle Robert's notes might give her the answer.

She went downstairs. Peter was waiting for her—the armchairs drawn up close to the flaming fire, a drink ready. He sat by her side and they talked. Lightly, amusingly as he told her of his interesting life and incidents that had happened to him during his working years abroad. It was a pleasant evening, only marred by Mrs. Stone's behaviour. The dinner was delicious, but she didn't say a word to Cindy. Cindy might just as well not have been there, she was so completely ignored while Mrs. Stone almost crawled at Peter's feet, determined to please him.

Afterwards as they drank their coffees by the fire, Peter looked at Cindy and grinned.

'Poor Mrs. Stone! Afraid of losing her job.'

'I suppose she is.' Cindy hadn't thought of that.

'What about your job? Have you lost it?'

'Oh no,' Cindy said eagerly. 'Mr. Jenkins said I could have a week off. I had some holiday time due.'

'A week? How long have you been here? One day to come up, two days here, so why not stay the whole week? As my guest, of course.'

Cindy stared at him. 'But why? I mean . . .'

'Because you love the Lake District and the castle. It may make your disappointment a little less painful. Besides, I'd be glad of your advice. Something must be done to make the castle habitable—new curtains and carpets and . . . Your advice would be of great help,' he added, and then smiled. 'Doesn't that sound pompous? Sorry, but I'd like you to stay.'

Cindy looked round the room wildly. Part of her longed to stay while the other part told her to run. And fast, too! This was the man she had fallen hopelessly in love with, the man she could not forget, and there could only be one result—heartache. Yet she wanted so badly to stay.

She was startled when he leaned forward and put his hand on hers. The touch of his warm fingers sent a tingling through her. 'Please!' he said quietly. 'It's years since I've been here and I'd enjoy driving round the Lakes with you. It's not much fun on your own.'

Staring at him as if mesmerised, Cindy swallowed.

'I'll stay,' she said. 'Just for the rest of the week.'

He let go her hand. 'Good! That calls for another drink.'

Later that night, in bed, Cindy read some more of Robert Baxter's notes. He blamed himself for losing his son, wished he could contact him and say how sorry he was, but the son never gave him an address, never approached him. Yet Luke Fairhead had said he'd seen Peter there! And Mr. Fairhead would not lie, Cindy thought.

Peter was already in the dining-room when Cindy went down for breakfast. He greeted her with a smile.

'Don't look as if you're on the way to the guillotine,' he said. 'I'm not going to eat you, you know.'

As usual, Cindy found herself laughing with him. 'I'm sorry, I didn't intend to look scared.'

Mrs. Stone came in with a big plate of sausages, bacon and eggs. She gave Cindy a strange look.

'You'll be packing to go now?' she asked, but it was more of a statement than a question.

Peter spoke before Cindy could. 'On the contrary, Mrs. Stone, Miss Preston has consented to stay for the rest of the week as my guest.'

Mrs. Stone looked startled. 'Is that so now?' she said, and almost scuttled from the room.

'Was Mrs. Stone here before you . . .' Cindy began, and then stopped, feeling her cheeks burn, for it was no business of hers and she had no desire to awaken sad memories.

But Peter didn't seem to mind. 'No,' he said,

69

'we had a dear old ex-nannie. You know the kind I mean. Unfortunately she died and I suppose my father engaged Mrs. Stone because he was sorry for her. My father was a strange man,' he went on as they ate their breakfast. 'The essence of compassion and understanding except where it concerned his son.'

Cindy looked at him quickly. 'Perhaps that was because he loved you.'

'Loved me? I doubt it,' said Peter. 'More coffee? Sleep all right?'

'Fine.' Cindy hesitated. Should she tell him about the diary she had found? Surely that would make him realise how much his father had loved him, and how greatly he regretted the quarrel? But Mrs. Stone came hustling back with some crisp hot toast.

'I hope it's all to your liking, Mr. Baxter,' she said.

Peter smiled at her. 'Splendid, Mrs. Stone, thanks.'

Mrs. Stone made a quick exit, giving a strange look in Cindy's direction.

'Why doesn't she like me?' Cindy asked.

Peter laughed. 'You're not as dumb as that, surely, Cindy? In the first place, she obviously expected the castle to be taken over by some wealthy person, so she hoped she could stay on . . . then you turn up, a bit of a girl without a penny, so she sees the sack—then she hears the castle is to be demolished, and then I turn

70

up. She must feel very confused and has to blame someone, and you happen to be handy.'

'I suppose that's one way of explaining it, but she hated me from the beginning . . . as they all do,' Cindy said wistfully.

'Can you blame them?' Peter frowned, rubbing his chin. Cindy realised suddenly that was a habit of his. She saw there was a cleft in his chin, or was it a dimple? He was looking at her with ill-concealed amusement and she felt her cheeks go hot.

'It wasn't my fault,' she said defiantly. 'Uncle Robert chose me. I didn't ask him to make me his second heir.'

'It wasn't that. It was the thought of the castle being pulled down and moved to another land.'

'That had nothing to do with me, either!' Cindy's voice rose angrily. 'I know you don't believe me, but it's the truth. I had no idea until you showed me the newspaper.'

He went on, half smiling at her in that hateful way.

'Is that so?' he said slowly.

Cindy's hand closed round the marmalade jar she happened to have in her hand. Never before had she so felt like throwing something at anyone. She put it down, stood up and said:

'I think it would be best if I leave at once.'

He stood up, too. 'I agree, provided we leave together in the same car.'

They stared at one another, Cindy clenching

71

and unclenching her hands. It wasn't right or fair for any man to be so handsome—to have those kind of eyes, that mouth . . .

'You did promise to stay,' Peter said gently.

Cindy swallowed. 'All right. I'd . . . I'd like to see Mrs. Usher.'

'Dear old Mrs. Usher? Is she still here?' Peter sounded pleased. 'I'd like to see her too. Look, I'll drop you there and go into the village as I have business to attend to and then I'll come back and pick you up? Okay?'

'Okay,' Cindy agreed, and went up to her room, changing into a pale yellow woollen frock, looking worriedly at her face half-hidden by her hair and glasses. He was being very pleasant, but at the same time she was conscious of this curtain between them—the curtain he had dropped because he could not—or would not—believe her.

Peter was waiting in front, wandering round. He looked up as she joined him.

'I don't think much of Paul Stone as a gardener, do you?'

'Well, I did think it looked pretty scruffy, but then I know nothing about gardening,' Cindy admitted as they got into the car.

'I'll have a talk with Luke Fairhead when we get back. Seems to me my father just gave up caring and the whole place has . . . well, gone to the dogs, you might say.'

Cindy looked at him quickly. There was an impatient note in his voice. He was probably

72

a hardworking perfectionist and expected everyone else to be the same. In that respect, he reminded her a little of her boss, Mr. Jenkins.

'I think Mrs. Stone has done a wonderful job,' she said quickly. 'It can't be easy to keep a place as big as the castle so clean and polished.'

Peter looked at her, his mouth curling a little. 'Yes, she's made a good job of it, but that doesn't excuse her son's laziness. Why do you want to see Mrs. Usher?' he asked abruptly.

'Because . . . because I like her.'

'That's not the truth, is it? You're a bad liar, Cindy,' Peter said, driving down the winding road towards the village. On the other side of the lake, lofty hills stood out boldly in the clear blue sky, that promised a perfect day.

'No,' Cindy agreed. 'I want to ask her advice.'

'Why not ask mine?'

Cindy turned towards him. 'Because you think I lied.'

'You didn't lie! I know that. I know you didn't write the article, but you could have known of the offer and accepted it—if the Castle became yours—before you ever came here. It was so obvious to me that Ayres was determined to make you sell the castle.'

'But he wasn't. He knew I wanted to live here.'

'Is that so?' Peter spoke slowly. 'You must

73

admit he made it plain that it would be impossible for you to afford it, didn't he?' He snapped the question at her.

Startled, Cindy said: 'Yes, but . . .'

'Look, there are too many "buts" for my liking. Ayres wanted you to see the castle—that we're agreed on. Right? Well, maybe Ayres arranged to sell it for you and someone sneaked out the news. Right?'

'No, definitely not right,' Cindy said quickly. 'Mr. Ayres isn't like that. He knew I was going to try everything to keep the castle.'

'And what, may I ask, is "everything"?'

Cindy's cheeks were hot. 'I thought perhaps it would make a hotel.'

'Ye gods and little fishes!' Peter nearly exploded. 'Just how naïve and stupid can you be? Have you any idea how much it costs to convert an old run-down place like it into a hotel?'

'We could have kept it as it is . . . people love to stay in a castle and they don't expect mod. cons. I believe they did it successfully in Ireland. People like to live as they did *then*!' Cindy fought back. 'And with the staff dressed in period clothes!'

He turned to look at her and laughed.

'Honestly, I didn't think people like you were still born. Where were you going to get the money?'

'That was what worried me,' Cindy said gravely. 'I wondered if the bank would loan it.'

They were near the village now, the blue water very still, the small snowdrops pushing up their white little heads above the soil. Peter left her at Mrs. Usher's cottage.

'I'll be along in about an hour, tell her,' he said, and drove away.

There was no answer to Cindy's knock. She waited, uncertain what to do, not wanting to go back to the village and the curious condemning eyes. Suddenly someone on a bicycle came along the road, stopped at the little wicket gate, and it was the little old lady who got off, waving a hand. She wore a trouser suit with a thick anorak and a scarf round her head.

'Well, dear, this is nice,' she smiled, lifting out her shopping. 'I had to go down along the lake to get my mushrooms. Do come in, the kettle will be boiling now.'

'I'm afraid it's very early.'

Mrs. Usher's face shone. 'The earlier the better, dear. Sit you down now and be comfy while I get around.'

In ten minutes the tea was ready, the fire crackling as Mrs. Usher looked at Cindy sympathetically.

'I thought maybe you'd come down now. ' 'Twas a nasty shock for you, I would say, seeing that in the paper.'

'Oh, Mrs. Usher!' For one awful moment, Cindy thought she was going to cry. 'You believe me, then? You know I had nothing to do with it?'

'Of course I do, child. ' 'Twouldn't be like you t'do such a thing. That's what I told them all. No judge of character, that's their trouble, as I said now. Tell me about it.'

Gratefully Cindy obeyed, starting with David Baxter waving the paper on the ferry.

'I thought he was the man I'd seen in London, but it seems he wasn't. Because Peter Baxter is quite different, yet they do look alike.'

'You thought David was Peter?' Mrs. Usher chuckled. 'I doubt if t'either would be flattered. Never did get on, those two.'

Then Cindy told Mrs. Usher of the scene in the post office.

'I could feel their anger and I didn't know what I'd done wrong.' She described her dismal day and how frightening the mountains and quiet lakes had been.

'I know, dear,' Mrs. Usher agreed. 'They can give you the creeps now. Real eerie, they are. So you went home.'

'Back to the castle, and . . . and he was there.'

Mrs. Usher's face dimpled as she tried not to laugh.

'And who, might I ask, is *he*?'

'Peter, of course.'

'Of course. Go on.'

So Cindy did; telling her how Peter had implied that she was lying, had said he planned

76

to let her have the castle until he saw the article in the paper.

'It isn't fair,' Cindy nearly wailed. 'I had nothing to do with the article. You know I would never sell the castle.'

'Unless you had no choice,' Mrs. Usher said dryly. 'Sometimes it's impossible to do what we want to. All the same, it is sad. You could have had the castle and Peter not had to come up. Is he sad about it? Memories?'

'He was and he isn't, if you know what I mean,' Cindy tried to explain. 'He's . . . well, not easy to understand. He's a mass of contradictions.'

Mrs. Usher poured them out more tea. 'He always was a strange one any time. So what happens now?'

'Well, I wanted to pack and go, because I have no right here now he's here and he wouldn't let . . .'

'Wouldn't let you?' Mrs. Usher looked shocked. 'You mean he stopped you?'

'In a way.' Cindy told the little old lady what had happened and was startled when Mrs. Usher laughed.

'The same old Peter—turns on the charm.' Suddenly she was serious. 'My dear child, don't tell me you've . . . ?'

Cindy knew instantly what she meant. 'I . . . I . . .'

'Am afraid so?' Mrs. Usher finished the sentence. 'Oh, my poor child! Peter isn't the marrying kind, you know.'

'I don't know, but I . . . well, I know he would never see me,' Cindy sighed.

'And why not?' Mrs. Usher's voice changed again; now it was sharp. 'You're a rare good-looking girl, my child, and don't forget it. There's a fey look about your face and dreamy eyes that has a charm all its own and . . .'

A knock on the door interrupted her and she got up to open it.

'Peter, my dear boy!' she exclaimed, putting her arms round him.

'Aunt Rhoda—it is good to see you!' he said warmly.

He came to sit by the fire while Mrs. Usher fluttered round like an anxious hen. 'I knew you'd be coming, Peter,' she said. 'And I cooked those crumpets you like. I'll go and fetch them now. I know you'll eat them any time.'

'You bet!' he grinned, and settled himself comfortably, stretching out his long legs, smiling at Cindy. 'Isn't she a pet?' he said softly.

Cindy nodded, her face grave. This was a different Peter from the one she knew. How relaxed he was, how . . . how happy.

Mrs. Usher joined them and she was full of questions. Where had Peter been; had he found the heat too much for him; any good adventures? How well he was looking and it was wonderful to have him back . . .

'Not that you were ever over-fond of this part of the world, Peter,' she said a little sadly. 'Nor was your mother, for that matter. It was your dad the castle meant so much to.'

'I know. That's why I'm here,' Peter said, looking across at Cindy, his eyes narrowed.

'Peter, I've known you since you were a small wee baby, so I can ask you certain things,' Mrs. Usher's face was concerned as she leant forward. 'Tell me. Peter, why didn't you write to your father?'

'But I did,' Peter said at once, leaning towards the old lady. 'That was the worst part of it. He returned every one of the letters. Unopened! Then I heard he was ill and I came across from Africa, came straight here. Mrs Stone went to tell him I was there and she came back and said he told her he never wanted to see me again. Mrs. Stone was upset and . . . and so was I.' He smiled ruefully. 'What more could I do, Aunt Rhoda? He just didn't want to have anything to do with me. That's why I was surprised when I heard he'd left everything to me.'

'Peter,' Cindy turned to him quickly, unable to keep quiet, 'the other day I found . . .'

There carne a pounding on the door and Mrs. Usher went to open it. Peter stood up as a tall girl came in. Cindy recognized her at once—Johanna Younge from the little tea-shop, the one-time beauty queen who had said jokingly that she was looking for a wealthy

79

husband.

Now she held out her hands. 'Welcome back, Peter. You won't remember me—we only met a few times.'

Peter smiled. 'Of course I do—the beauty queen. We all envied Jim and wondered how he'd done it.'

'You're back for good?' Johanna said eagerly.

'In a sense. I'll be here some time, anyhow,' Peter told her.

Johanna smiled at Cindy. 'Tough luck, Miss Preston, but the castle needs a man. It'll be nice having you around, Peter, one gets very bored here.' She gave him a brilliant smile, then looked at Mrs. Usher. 'Just thought I'd pop in and welcome him back.'

'Very sweet of you, dear, most thoughtful,' Mrs. Usher said, her voice dry. She closed the door and smiled at Peter. 'Well?'

'She hasn't changed at all, has she?' he said, and laughed. 'Once a beauty queen, always a beauty queen, I suppose. Well, Cindy, it's a lovely morning. I suggest we drive around and share the beauty.'

'A good idea,' Mrs. Usher said warmly. 'It really is nice to have you back, Peter.'

He bent and kissed her lightly. 'Know something, Aunt Rhoda? It's nice to be back, too.'

Once in the car, he looked at Cindy.

'I meant it,' he said. 'I wasn't happy here

80

before—perhaps that's why I hated the place. Today I can see its charm.'

It was a pleasant morning. Peter took her to see all the beauty he found himself remembering. They stopped at Ambleside and looked at the quaint little cottage perched on the bridge, he showed her Cray Castle and then the cottage where Wordsworth lived and the rock on which he was supposed to have sat as he composed his poems, as well as the church where he and so many of his family were buried. Finally Peter drove then into the more bleak mountains, explaining that screes were where rocks had broken into small fragments and were dangerous to walk on. He showed her the majestic beauty of Honister Pass and the gloomy frightening greyness of Wastwater. As they drove back to Claife Castle, Cindy felt sad, for she had an intuition that this would be their last morning alone together. She didn't know why, but she had a feeling that something unpleasant was about to happen . . .

As they went into the Castle Mrs. Stone came hurrying, her face concerned.

'You're late now, and a young lady phoned you, Mr. Baxter, asked you to pick her up at the station.'

'A young lady?' Peter sounded perplexed and then he laughed. 'Was her name by chance Miss Todd?' he said.

'That's right.'

81

'Well, we're starving, so please serve lunch, Mrs. Stone. Paul can fetch the young lady.'

'But she won't have had anything to eat.'

'I expect she's eaten there. In any case, she's on a diet, so it won't hurt her to starve for once—or if she's hungry when she arrives, I'm sure you can toss up a delectable omelette.' He smiled as he spoke, but Cindy shivered. She knew—how she had no idea—but she knew he was angry, that he was battling to control his temper.

Who was this Miss Todd? Cindy wondered as they ate their lunch almost in silence. He didn't seem to want to talk, so she sat quietly.

They were drinking coffee when they heard the sound of a car. Peter frowned and looked at Cindy.

'Women!' he said scathingly. 'Why were they ever invented? They're nothing but a nuisance!'

CHAPTER SEVEN

They sat in silence, listening to the impatient hammering on the front door, then the squeak as it was opened.

Cindy had no idea what sort of person she expected 'Miss Todd' to be, but it seemed obvious that she was someone Peter didn't like particularly, for he had sent Paul to meet her, and also told Mrs. Stone they wouldn't wait for lunch! So, as Cindy heard the sound of heels pattering on the polished floor, an impatient voice and Mrs. Stone's shrill answer before the dining-room door was flung open and 'Miss Todd' stood there, she hadn't expected what she saw!

Cindy caught her breath; for a moment she could not believe her eyes or that this slim, tall, beautiful girl could possibly be 'Miss Todd'.

But she obviously was, for Peter was on his feet.

'Hullo, Yvonne.'

She practically charged into the room, glaring at him, her black and white fur coat swinging, her small white fur hat perched on top of short curly dark hair.

'I just can't understand you, Peter Baxter!' she almost shouted, her cheeks flushed with rage. 'A fine way to treat me! I had to wait on that beastly cold platform—I'm starving, and then, to add to it, you haven't the decency to come and meet me yourself!' She looked round the room and as she saw Cindy, she seemed to freeze with shock, then swung round to look at Peter.

'What's *she* doing here? I'd have thought she'd have the decency to go after the way she's behaved!' Yvonne Todd demanded.

Peter's face was suddenly hard. 'Miss Preston was a good friend of my father's and I hope she will be my friend, too, so kindly stop behaving like a fishwife and being so rude!'

Peter and the lovely girl just stood and stared at one another—almost as if it was the start of a duel, Cindy thought, as she stood up. Or perhaps two angry cats about to fight.

Yvonne gave a little grunt, then smiled politely. 'How do you do, Miss Preston. Delighted to meet you,' she said sarcastically before turning back to Peter. 'What some people can get away with amazes me. You're just like your father—soft to the wrong people. Is that boy bringing in my luggage?'

Peter raised an eyebrow. 'You've come to stay?'

'Of course. You'll need a woman's hand here.' She looked round the lofty cold room and at the big oil paintings on the wall. 'It has gone to seed, hasn't it? I can't wait to explore it.' She turned swiftly to Cindy, her eyes bright with suspicion. 'I suppose you've been over it

84

from top to toe with a magnifying glass,' Yvonne Todd added bitterly.

'Naturally Cindy was interested in what she believed might be her castle,' Peter said quietly.

Cindy wondered what she should do. Her inclination was to rush out of the room, for why should she stand there to be insulted? Yet Peter was defending her . . . it was puzzling. Yvonne Todd was everything Cindy wished she could be—tall, slim, those huge dark eyes, the high cheekbones, the husky voice . . .

'Mrs. Stone will show you to a room,' Peter said, turning to the tall thin silent woman who was still standing just outside the door, her eyes bright with curiosity. 'I'm sorry at such short notice, Mrs. Stone, but I wasn't expecting Miss Todd.'

Cindy saw the colour flame in Yvonne's cheeks and the quick intake of breath she gave. So Yvonne Todd *had* come up uninvited?

'Yvonne,' Peter swung round, 'if you're hungry, I'm sure Mrs. Stone would make you an omelette. I understood you were on a diet.' He looked at his watch. 'I must go. I have an appointment with Mr. Fairhead.' He glanced at Cindy. 'I'm sure you can find plenty to do and I imagine Yvonne will be busy unpacking her incredible amount of luggage, so I suggest we all meet for tea.'

He walked past Yvonne, who took a step

back, showing her surprise. Cindy hurried after him, trying to get to the stairs. She was going to start packing immediately, and while Peter was with Mr. Fairhead, she could quietly slip away.

But at the foot of the stairs, Peter caught her by the arm. 'I'm sorry, Cindy, for her rudeness. Yvonne believes in calling a spade a spade.'

Cindy looked at him. 'She doesn't just call a spade a spade, she . . .' she stopped herself in time. What was the good of losing her temper? It wouldn't help. She looked up at him. 'Look, Peter, I think it would be better for us all if I go back to London. I can always sleep on the way if it gets foggy, as I did coming up.'

He looked at her, his thick eyebrows moving together.

'You promised,' he said gently. 'I had an idea you always kept your word.'

'But . . . but you don't need me now. You have her.'

'Suppose I don't want her?'

Cindy managed to laugh. 'Please! Look, I'm sure I'll only be in the way . . .'

His hand tightened on her arm. 'Please,' he echoed.

She sighed, 'All right . . .'

'Good girl! See you later,' Peter smiled, and hurried out of the front door while Cindy, giving a quick glance at the five enormous suitcases piled up in the hall, fled up the stairs.

86

How long did Yvonne Todd propose to stay? she wondered. How close were Yvonne and Peter? He had been almost rude and she had been angry in a possessive way. It seemed to be a strange sort of . . . well, relationship.

Alone in her bedroom, Cindy locked the door, got out Uncle Robert's diary, curled up on the windowsill, the electric fire switched on and a blanket round her shoulders, for the rooms were too big to heat quickly.

She read slowly the tiny beautifully written words, because it was difficult. It seemed odd that a successful business man who was, apparently, rather a tyrant could have written with such care, obviously thinking about each word before he wrote it.

It was sad reading. He admitted frankly that he regretted so much of his past. He wrote of his wife, 'so gentle that it irritated me immensely',—of his son, 'too much like me. Maybe that is why we constantly clashed.'

Cindy was searching for the mention of his illness, of the day his son had come to see him and he had rejected him, telling Mrs. Stone to tell his son that he never wanted to see him again.

Somehow it didn't make sense—unless this *diary* was supposed to be a satire? Could it be that he had written it as a joke? Pretending to be the opposite of everything he was. Or was this his real self?

He had written down the dates he wrote, so

perhaps if she could find out *when* Peter had come to see his father, she could trace the entry Uncle Robert would have surely made? Mrs. Stone might know, but she was the last person Cindy wanted to ask. Peter? Definitely no. That left her Luke Fairhead. He had said he had *seen* Peter—even if it wasn't the actual date, he might remember the year and the season which would help.

Quickly Cindy locked away Uncle Robert's diary, brushed her hair, put on a warm yellow jersey over blue trousers. If she was quick, she might catch Mr. Fairhead after his talk with Peter. She would wait in the car . . . from there she could see Mr. Fairhead's office. He was sure to be there before going home.

The castle was very still as Cindy went down the curving staircase as quietly as she could, for she had no desire to meet Yvonne Todd. The drawing-room was empty, so she let herself out through one of the french windows on to the paved terrace that ran down the sides of the castle. Even as she did, a man came out from the shadow of a clump of trees and came to meet her.

A short man, not much taller than herself, Cindy noticed. He had a pointed black beard, sideboards and even thicker black eyebrows than Peter.

'Miss Preston?' he said politely.

'Yes.' She was startled. There was no sign of a car, so how had he got up there? Unless he had parked the car further down the road and came up quietly, not wanting to be seen. But if so . . .

'I understand you are inheriting this castle,' he went on.

Cindy stared at him and frowned. 'I am not. Mr. Baxter's son is.'

'I understand he can't be traced.'

'He's been found. He's here now,' Cindy told him. 'Look, I'm afraid I can't stop now . . .'

The man moved forward, blocking her way. 'Please, Miss Preston. You say Peter Baxter has been found? This is news. So the castle and its treasures are no longer yours. Is Mr. Baxter here?'

'Yes. Look, I can't . . .'

'Mr. Baxter is staying here and so are you?' The short man grinned, his big white teeth flashing. 'Oh, maybe you and he will marry and share the castle?' He gave a funny little laugh.

'It's most unlikely,' Cindy said angrily. 'We don't know one another. Besides, he has a friend also staying . . .' She stopped abruptly. She shouldn't be answering questions. It would only mean more *news* in the papers and more trouble.

'I see . . . the eternal triangle!' he chuckled, and Cindy's cheeks burned.

'Look, please get out of my way. I don't wish to be interviewed.'

'I understand. You've found yourself in a

89

very embarrassing position, Miss Preston. I understand you arranged to sell the castle to an American. Will Mr. Baxter do the same?'

'What the . . .' Peter had come round the side of the castle and towered above them. 'Just who are you?' he asked angrily. 'You know Miss Preston?'

The little man swung round. 'She spoke to me on the phone in London.'

'I did not!' Cindy cried.

Both the men looked at her.

'Excuse me, Miss Preston, but you did. You rang my newspaper and told me about the castle you were about to inherit and that you'd been made an offer by an American which you were going to accept if the deceased's son did not turn up . . .' the little man said quietly.

Cindy stared at him, bewildered. Suddenly she thought of something. 'I gave you my name?'

He shook his head. 'I asked, but you said you'd prefer not to . . .'

'Why should I have said that? What did it matter if you had my name?' Cindy asked quickly. 'You could easily have found out from the solicitor . . .'

'Ah, the solicitor,' Peter said.

Cindy looked up at him. 'Peter, I didn't phone the newspaper. Why should I? It just doesn't make sense . . .'

It certainly didn't. Peter soon got rid of the polite little reporter who told them his name was Neil Gifford and he was sorry if he had embarrassed them but . . . news was news and it was his job. He finally went and Cindy looked at Peter who looked back at her, an odd expression on his face.

'You don't believe me, do you?' Cindy said. 'This is the end. I'm going . . .'

He caught her by both arms. 'Oh, no, you're not,' he said quietly. 'Not until I say so . . .'

She tried to free herself, but his grip was tight.

'There's something funny here,' he told her. 'And you're not going until I find out . . .'

'Peter . . .' A demanding voice broke the stillness as they looked at one another. 'Peter . . . where are you . . .'

Yvonne came round the corner, elegant in her white trouser suit. 'Oh, there you are,' she said, her voice disapproving. 'What's going on?'

'I've just persuaded Cindy to stay on. She's eager to get back to London, but I said we would prefer her to stay.' Peter gave an odd smile. 'We need a chaperone.'

He let go of Cindy and they walked back to the front of the castle. Mrs. Stone must have seen the french window open, for now it was closed and locked and they heard the tinkle of a gong through the open front door.

'Tea,' said Peter. 'I don't know about you two, but I could do with a cup.' He looked at Cindy. 'Things are worse than I expected them

91

to be, according to Luke Fairhead. I imagine you saw that, too.'

Yvonne, leading the way, spoke over her shoulder.

'Surely your father was a rich man? I understood . . .' She stopped abruptly. 'Who was that little man I saw walking down the drive?'

'Only a reporter,' Cindy said.

'A reporter?' There was a sharp note in Yvonne's voice. 'What was he doing here?'

'Asking questions, of course. That's what reporters always do,' Peter told her, his voice amused.

'I know that,' Yvonne snapped. 'But what about?'

'The American who wants to buy the castle and take it, stone by stone, to rebuild in his own country,' Peter said slowly, sounding bored.

'Well, that's off now, isn't it?' said Yvonne. 'So it isn't news.'

'Isn't it?' said Peter, as they reached the open front door where Mrs. Stone stood, tall, dignified and disapproving, the gong in her hands. 'I wonder . . .' he added as he led the way indoors.

CHAPTER EIGHT

Tea was not a very pleasant meal for Cindy, as Yvonne completely ignored her, talking to Peter all the time while Peter kept including Cindy in the conversation. Afterwards, Peter looked at Yvonne.

'Like me to show you round the castle?' he asked casually.

'I have been all over it, but maybe you'll show me things I missed,' Yvonne said with a sweet smile.

'Good—let's go, now.' Peter got up and they left the room. Cindy sat very still, trying to reassure herself that Peter hadn't just forgotten her, that he might have done it thoughtfully, in believing that it would be kinder not to show her the castle she had lost.

Mrs. Stone came in to collect the tea things. She gave Cindy a quick, disapproving glance but said nothing. Cindy went up to her bedroom and got out Uncle Robert's diary. If only she knew the date of the day Mr. Fairhead had seen Peter come to see his father! Suddenly she knew what she must do. Quickly she put away the notes, pulled on her anorak, because it would be chilly outside, and hurried out to Mr. Fairhead's office.

He wasn't there. But Paul Stone was. He looked up from some bushes he was clipping and asked her what she wanted.

'I want to see Mr. Fairhead.'

'Why?' he asked.

Cindy bit her lip. 'That's my business.'

'No longer,' Paul Stone said with a grin. 'How do you feel now?' He laughed. 'Serves you right, that's what I say.'

'Look, Mr. Stone,' Cindy kept a grip on her temper, 'I want to see Mr. Fairhead. Where would he be at this time?'

Paul Stone made a great show of looking at his watch. He took as long as he could over it, even lifting it to his ear to see if it was ticking. Cindy forced herself to wait. She had to see Luke Fairhead, otherwise she would have walked off.

'Reckon that at this hour, he'll be home with his missus. It's other side of the village. You can't mistake it, t'roof is going green with age.'

'Thank you,' Cindy said politely. 'I'll wait and see him tomorrow.'

Paul grinned. 'He won't be coming tomorrow, neither the next day. He has his own farm to run.'

'I see.' Cindy hesitated for a moment, then went and backed her car out. It was fast growing dark, but that didn't worry her.

She had soon driven through the village. There was an open space of fields coming down to the lakeside and then she saw a large square-looking farmhouse. She couldn't see if the roof was green or not, but she pulled up outside and went through the little white gate to the front door. She pulled the bell and the door opened. A tall woman with a large plump face and a friendly smile stared at her. She wore a bright blue frock.

'Who's ta wanting?' she asked.

'Is this Mr. Fairhead's farm?' Cindy was relieved when the woman nodded. 'I wonder if I could see him.'

'Of course.' The door was opened wider and she was invited into a tiled hall. 'You must be Miss Preston. Luke is just having tea. Come and join us, Miss Preston.'

'That's very good of you.'

'A pleasure, I'm sure. I'm Mrs. Fairhead, Maidie Fairhead. Born in this house, and so was my grandfather,' she said as she led the way down the hall and to a huge warm kitchen where a kitchen range blazed cheerfully.

Mr. Fairhead stood up. He was in his shirt sleeves and looked a little embarrassed. Two or three children were also at the table and turned to stare at Cindy.

'Come in, Miss Preston,' Luke Fairhead said warmly. 'Sit down and have something to eat.'

'No, thanks. I've just had tea,' Cindy smiled at him. 'I tried to see you before you left the castle, but I got held up.'

Luke Fairhead grinned. 'The Press, I hear. Peter Baxter wasn't amused, eh?'

Cindy laughed. 'Nor was I. Why can't the

Press leave us alone?' She sat back in the high-backed chair and ran her hand over her face. 'You know, Mr. Fairhead, sometimes I wish Uncle Robert *had* forgotten me.'

Mrs. Fairhead leaned forward eagerly. 'I remember when you stayed at the castle with your mum. A lovely woman, she. You were but a little lass.'

'I loved the castle. It was so . . . so . . .'

'Romantic,' Luke Fairhead said drily.

Cindy looked at him ruefully. 'I still find it fascinating. Will . . . will Peter be able to save it?'

'I think so. Shrewd, that lad's become. And bright. I always thought he was. Eeeh, Miss Preston, maybe I shouldn't ask you any time, but . . . but is he, and that . . . well . . .' Luke Fairhead seemed embarrassed and looked at his wife. She came to the rescue.

'We were wondering, like, if he was going to marry Miss Todd any time.'

Cindy looked at them both and shook her head. 'I don't know. She practically told me they were.'

'And what did he say, Peter himself?' Luke Fairhead asked.

'He wasn't there. I don't know him very well. I mean, we've only just met and . . .'

Maidie Fairhead nodded her head wisely, her dark hair slightly streaked with grey. 'A good-looking lad is our Peter. ' 'Twas a sad day when he left. I always wished he and his dad could have made it up. Fair broke his dad's heart, it did.'

Cindy drank the cup of tea she had been given, then turned to Luke Fairhead. 'Can you remember when it was that Peter came to see his father and was turned away?'

Luke's weatherbeaten face wrinkled as he frowned.

'Ah'll think. Maidie, you're the one for remembering . . . Let's see, he died three years ago, and ' 'twas about a year before.'

'It was September four years ago. I remember how upset you were, Luke. Fair broke your heart.'

'Well, the look on that lad's face . . .'

'It couldn't have been easy for Mrs. Stone to have to give Peter the message,' Cindy said, and saw the quick look the two Fairheads gave one another. 'You said the quarrel broke his dad's heart, yet he refused to see Peter. It doesn't make sense.'

'You're right. We couldn't understand it. Mrs. Stone, none of us liked her any time. Just crazy about that boy of hers, out to get all she could from the poor old man . . .'

'Do you think . . .' Cindy began cautiously. 'Do you think Mrs. Stone could have made it up and actually never told Uncle Robert that Peter had come to see him?'

Again Mr. and Mrs. Fairhead glanced at one another.

'Wouldn't put it past her,' said Mrs.

97

Fairhead. 'We never did trust her. Luke's always saying the money she spent on running the Castle and we couldn't see where t'had gone.'

'You'll be leaving us soon?' Luke Fairhead asked. 'I'm sorry.'

Cindy smiled at him. 'Thanks very much. I'm sorry, too, but I always did know that if Peter turned up, the castle wouldn't be mine. You know, it's strange. I just can't understand it, but . . . but Peter was going to let me have the castle, he said, because he didn't want it and he knew I did, but . . . but then there was that article in the paper. You saw it, of course?'

The children had raced away with Bessie, the dog, and now there was only Cindy and the two Fairheads round the table.

'I didn't give that information to the paper. I knew nothing about it,' Cindy said almost desperately. 'And today that horrible little reporter came and asked questions and told Peter I'd phoned him and told him about the American offer. I knew nothing about it.'

Luke Fairhead leaned forward and patted her hand. 'Don't fret so, lass. We know that.'

'Peter doesn't believe me.' Cindy heard the desperate note in her voice and stopped.

'Another cup of tea, love?' Mrs. Fairhead asked tactfully, rising to take the cup and fill it.

'That doesn't sound like our Peter,' commented Luke.

'Well, as I said, the reporter told Peter *I* had phoned him and told him that if I inherited the castle I would sell it to the American, and I didn't.' Again, Cindy heard her voice rise.

Mrs. Fairhead put the cup of tea on the table. 'There, love, don't let it fret you. I'm sure no one with sense would believe you'd do a thing like that.'

'Peter does,' said Cindy, and sipped the hot sweet tea gratefully.

Afterwards she told them about the diary she had found.

'I felt rather awful about reading it, but . . . but I wanted to know more about Uncle Robert and . . . and honestly, he seemed awfully upset about Peter and blamed himself.'

'Has Peter read it?' Luke asked.

'Not yet. I'm giving it to him when I leave at the end of the week because I haven't finished it. It's terribly tiny writing and I'm afraid Peter might be too impatient to read it and miss the important parts. About the letters, I mean. Peter told me that he got back all the letters he wrote to his father, they were returned unopened. Yet Uncle Robert says how he longs for a letter. And I want to see if I can trace the entry of September, four years ago, and see what he says then about Peter's visit. I can't understand why he refused to see Peter when he kept writing about him.'

'*If* . . . he refused,' Maidie Fairhead said slowly. 'I never did trust that Stone woman.'

'You think she may have?' Cindy looked at them. 'I want to be able to say to Peter, read these dates and see what your father really felt. As I said, the writing is terribly small and Peter can be impatient.' She smiled. 'Oh, I can't tell you how wonderful it is to have you both on my side. I wanted to leave, but Peter persuaded me to stay, and yet I feel horribly in the way and . . . and unwanted. It hurts when someone you . . . when someone just refuses to believe you,' she added wistfully.

'We're behind you all the way,' Luke Fairhead said gravely. 'Maybe you've mistook Peter. ' 'Twasn't the impression I got.'

The grandfather clock in the hall chimed noisily.

'I'd better go.' Cindy jumped up. 'If I'm late for dinner, it'll just give them something else to blame me for.'

Both Fairheads went out to see Cindy off in her little grey car.

'Thanks . . . thanks for everything,' Cindy called.

Driving back to the castle, she felt happier than she had done for days, for at least the Fairheads were on her side.

Peter was in the hall and opened the door after she had knocked.

'Where have you been?' he asked angrily. 'You had me worried.'

'I wanted to see Mr. Fairhead.'

'Was it important?' Peter demanded.

Cindy looked up at him. Should she tell him, now? she wondered. Or would it be better to wait until she could give specific facts and dates to look up?

'Yes, it was,' she said coldly, and walked by him. 'I think I'll have an early night. I'm tired.'

'Come and have a drink,' he said, taking her anorak off and leading the way to the drawing-room.

Yvonne glanced up from where she sat by the fire.

'I thought you'd gone,' she said, her voice implying that it was a pity Cindy hadn't.

The Fairheads' loyalty and belief in her had heightened Cindy's courage, so she laughed:

'I promised Peter I'd stay till the end of the week.'

Yvonne frowned. 'It seems daft to me, it can only hurt you more.'

'On the contrary,' Cindy said almost light-heartedly, 'I'm thoroughly enjoying it.'

After dinner, they were having coffee in the drawing-room and talking when Mrs. Stone opened the door and said, her voice stiff:

'Mr. Baxter . . . Mr. David Baxter.'

Cindy looked up, startled, staring at the man she had mistaken for Peter. Now she saw the two of them together, she could see how foolish she had been.

'David!' Peter stood up and went, hand outstretched. The two men stood side by side, so alike and yet so completely different.

Peter's skin was sun-tanned whereas David's was florid. Peter's hair was cut short whereas David's was much longer, curling slightly. Peter's smile was friendly—David's sour.

'I thought I'd better look in and welcome you home,' he said.

'I'm glad you did. Look, Yvonne, I want you to meet my cousin, David.'

David smiled more graciously as he nodded to Yvonne, whose face had brightened when she saw him.

'And this is Cindy. I think you've met.' Peter's voice rippled with laughter.

'Met?' David frowned. 'Not exactly.'

Peter had to laugh. 'She thought you were me.'

'She did?' David looked startled. 'That explains . . .'

Cindy pushed her glasses up a little. 'Yes, I thought you were Peter that day you bumped into me at the post office.'

'We're not alike,' David told her quickly.

'We are in a way,' said Peter. 'Cindy, when she first met me, wasn't wearing her glasses, so she didn't really know what I looked like.'

David began to laugh and the two men, looking at Cindy, laughed together. Yvonne sat quietly, looking disdainfully away from Cindy as if Cindy had done something offensive.

'I forgot them that day.'

'I know,' said Peter. 'You were so excited.

102

Anyhow, what about a drink, David? Sit down. It's been a long time.'

'You knew I bought your father's business?' David asked, sitting next to Yvonne but looking at Peter who was handling the bottles.

'I didn't, but I was told since I got back.'

'Your father aged fast. I think he was relieved when I took over.'

'How's it doing?'

'Fine, just fine,' David said, but the bitterness in his voice shocked Cindy.

'Yvonne here is a good business woman,' said Peter, coming to sit in the circle. 'She started off with one boutique in Sydney—we met in Australia—did so well, she had one in every city, then moved over here. Already she's got three going in England, haven't you, Yvonne?'

David was looking impressed.

'You came over together?'

'No, but we're old friends, aren't we, Yvonne?' Peter said with a strange smile, 'always meeting by chance.'

Cindy wondered why Yvonne was frowning. Peter went on: 'Actually Yvonne has lucky fingers. Everything she touches succeeds. Remember the old legend of Midas? How everything he touched turned to gold? Yvonne is like that, but it isn't all luck, she has brains and the ability to judge characters.'

'Better than you, Peter,' said Yvonne, almost snapping as if he was annoying her.

'She should have been a man,' Peter went on. 'She'd have ended up as a business tycoon, a millionaire. I'm not sure she isn't headed that way already. She's a real genius—she has the gift of choosing the right people for the jobs and keeping an eye on them so that things don't go wrong.'

David looked even more impressed. 'You like England?'

'I think there are terrific opportunities here for anyone who works hard and has a bit of initiative,' Yvonne said, giving Cindy a quick glance, almost, Cindy thought, as if suggesting that Cindy lacked the latter, so could never be a success.

'I'm thinking of giving a party, David. I hope you'll come,' Peter announced.

'I'd like to, thanks. When?'

'It has to be this week, because we're losing Cindy.' Peter said casually. 'Make it Friday?'

'Fine.' David stood up. 'I must be going now. Nice meeting you,' he said, smiling at Yvonne.

Cindy seized her opportunity to slip away to her bedroom as Peter walked out with David to his car. Hurriedly she undressed and got into bed, Uncle Robert's diary in her hand.

September, four years ago . . .

It was difficult to find, but finally she got near the mark. September 28th.

'Sometimes Mrs. Stone is a menace. She is convinced I have bronchitis threatening and

104

insists I stay in bed. I am not feeling well and very exhausted, so instead of losing my temper, I agreed, just to keep the peace. I find it very lonely, for I miss my chats with Luke. He never attempts to see me, nor do I have any visitors at all. Mrs. Stone has a poor opinion of my neighbours, such as they are. She says that not even in the village does anyone enquire after me. I suppose one must expect this as one grows older and of less use. At the same time, it hurts.'

Cindy sighed with relief. She had found what she wanted to find. She scrambled out of bed, hunting for pencil and paper, finally finding it, writing on the paper: 'Dear Peter. You never believe me, so you may not believe me now, but please read page 33. This was the time you came to see your father. I don't believe Mrs. Stone ever told him you were here. If you can read it all, you'll see he never got your letters. I think Mrs. Stone may have sent them back to you. Ask Mrs. Usher. She'll tell you that Mrs. Stone hoped your father would leave the castle to Paul—perhaps that was why she kept you apart.'

She sighed, folded and put it in the notebook. She would give it to Peter as she left and leave him to decide what to do . . .

As she fell asleep, she felt happier. At least when Peter read the notes he would realise that his father had not stopped loving him as he had thought.

CHAPTER NINE

When Cindy awoke, the sun was shining. She rose early and hurried down to be the first at breakfast. When Yvonne and Peter joined her, she was finishing her second cup of coffee.

'Isn't it a lovely day?' she said, smiling at them. 'I'm going for a long walk.'

Peter looked sceptical. 'Watch out for the screes, and don't get lost. If a mist comes down . . .'

'Really, Peter,' Yvonne interrupted, 'she isn't a child!'

Cindy stood up. One of these days, she knew she was going to lose her temper with Yvonne. 'See you at lunch,' she said, and hurried away, going to her room to change into jeans and her warm anorak, brushing back her hair and tying it loosely with ribbon.

Then she set off. It was so beautiful that she was glad she was alone—for such beauty required you to sit and enjoy it without interruption. Perched on a boulder, she looked down at the castle below. How huge it seemed from here with its tall square castellated towers, the funny little slits of windows in them, the courtyard in the middle. For a moment, tears stung her eyes. She wished she had never seen the castle again. Before it had been a child's dream—now it was real.

Yet in a way she was glad she had come. Despite the unhappy moments, she would never forget her week up here.

Was it because of Peter? she asked herself. Each time she saw him, she loved him more. How could she ever get over it? Did people get over broken hearts or did the pain stay for ever?

She began to walk again, finding the paths that wound round the hillside, pausing to look at the streams trickling down towards the lake. She walked over to the other side where she could no longer be tempted to keep stopping to stare down at the castle, and found something beautiful. It was an immense waterfall, the water sliding abruptly over the side of huge polished boulders, falling far below into a pool, where the water frothed before escaping into a brook that weaved its way between small trees and foliage, yet still made its way to the lake. Above the waterfall was a huge erect boulder and a flat one before it on which one could stand, gazing down the long drop into the white-frothed water.

Sitting down, she looked at it. How quiet everything was save for the distant cries of the gulls and the sound of water. When she heard a scraping noise, she turned, startled.

Peter!

'Hi,' he said, lifting his hand. 'Mind if I join you?'

'Of course not.' She was puzzled. 'Yvonne?'

'Didn't feel like walking. Wants to go over the castle again.' He frowned. 'I can't understand her interest in it. I mean, it isn't as if it was a *real* castle—that would be understandable because of its age and association with people dead for hundreds of years, but why *this* castle? I think she's been right through it several times already, yet she's still fascinated. Now she's down in the vaults, she says they would make good playrooms—billiards, table tennis, etc.'

'But wouldn't that spoil the atmosphere? I mean, if people are . . . are coming to live in an *old* castle, surely they wouldn't expect modern games and things?'

Peter shrugged. 'I agree with you. Of course, on the other hand, Yvonne is right. We have to think of the financial side of it. Why did you want to see Luke?' he asked abruptly. 'Was it about me?'

Startled, Cindy looked at him, then away. 'Not really.'

'Then why did you want to see him?'

'It was something he'd told me about Uncle Robert . . . I wanted to make sure I'd remembered right.'

'Look, let's get things in proportion. You met my father when you were seven or eight. How long did you stay here?'

'I don't know. It didn't seem long enough to me.'

'Why did he ask you?'

'Mrs. Usher said he wanted to marry my mother. She . . . she didn't like the castle and nothing would have made your father move.'

Peter laughed. 'Odd to think that I might have been your stepbrother.'

Cindy gave him a quick glance. Perhaps it would have been better that way, then she wouldn't have loved him. Or would she? It might have made it even more complicated.

'Anyhow, Cindy, let's face it. You were only with my father for a few weeks. You can't be so interested in him.'

Cindy swung round. 'But I can! Don't you see, Peter, how wonderful it was to me to know your father had never forgotten me? I mean . . . it probably doesn't worry a man, but . . . but I was very much alone after Mummy died and I was miserable living with my aunts, uncles and cousins. Then . . . then just before I got the letter, I'd been given the brush-off.'

'Brush-off?'

'Yes. Oliver . . . oh, I know it wasn't anything much, but he seemed to like me and took me out and then dropped me. I was . . . well, pretty upset, and . . . and I felt no one cared what happened to me, and then this letter came and Uncle Robert had never forgotten me, he cared . . . he knew I would love the castle and look after it for him.'

'I see.' Peter was silent for a moment. 'You do love this part of the world. I'd forgotten how beautiful it was.'

109

Cindy, glad that the subject had been changed, turned to him again. 'There are so many words I don't understand. What is a fell?'

'I suppose you could call it a mountain or large hill. Dales are the valleys. Mere means water. Windermere and all the other names come from that.'

'I saw a strange name the other day—Ings. I.N.G.S.'

Peter chuckled. 'It does sound crazy, doesn't it? Actually it means *fields with water.*'

'Everything is so quiet here, no people, no mad rush of cars.'

'That's because it's winter. I bet it's very different in summer. Tourists pour in. Then of course there are masses of climbers and walkers. Place is packed with young walkers and lots of hostels for them. Then the birds . . . It isn't nearly so quiet then.'

'But even that couldn't change its beauty,' Cindy persisted.

Peter laughed, 'You have got the bug all right! What do you think of this waterfall? Did you stand on the rock?'

'No, I'm not good at heights. It's terrific though.'

'There's a legend about it. Apparently in 1806 a young girl came to stay in the village. She was alone and in those days young women rarely travelled or lived on their own. Her landlady asked questions, but the girl evaded

110

them all. Every day she went to walk on the fells. Always she wore a white dress with broad pink ribbons tied round the waist, with two long ends dangling at the back and reaching to her feet. Then she would stand on a rock and let the wind blow the ribbons round her. This was her favourite place and she would stand on that rock, gazing down at the water below, the ribbons fluttering in the wind.' He laughed. 'You can imagine the gossip in the village, but she ignored it. Then one day a carriage was seen, but it vanished almost as fast. The girl never came home that night from the fells, nor was she ever seen again or her body found. No one *knew* what had happened. Some people said that someone must have come in the carriage to fetch her, others that she had jumped into the water in despair. It was even suggested that someone who came in the carriage had crept up behind her and pushed her in. Mrs. Usher used to tell me that story when I was very young. I could never understand why she wept. Maybe it was an ancestor of hers.'

Cindy stared at the huge erect pillar of rock, imagining the girl standing there, leaning against it, looking down at the water foaming so far below. Had she jumped to escape the sorrow she couldn't bear any more? Maybe she had felt as Cindy did—the hopeless pain of loving a man who loved another.

She shivered. 'What a sad story! Perhaps we

should be going back.' She jumped up. He did the same, standing by her side.

'Cindy,' he said abruptly, 'could you be a little more friendly to Yvonne?'

She was so startled that she nearly lost her balance, but he caught her by the arm.

'Watch out! You could have fallen in.'

They walked slowly down the path that led back to the castle's track.

'Yvonne is hurt by your behaviour,' he began, and when she looked up at him, frowning, her eyes puzzled, he burst out laughing. 'Sorry, I did sound pompous, didn't I? Yvonne has that effect on me. She should have been born a hundred years ago.'

'I think if anyone could be hurt, it should be me,' Cindy said angrily. 'She isn't exactly friendly, so why should I be?'

'Because she can't help it. Jealousy is a disease, something that isn't her fault. We should feel sorry for her.'

'Jealous?' Cindy almost laughed. 'Who of? Certainly not me.'

'You're wrong. She is jealous of you— bitterly.'

Cindy stopped dead and turned to face him. 'But how can she be when she has everything I would like? She's so tall and graceful and beautiful and . . .'

'Boring,' Peter ended. 'All Yvonne thinks about is money.'

'How can you say such a horrible thing when

112

she's your . . .'

'Maybe because I know her so well. That's not her fault either. She needs financial security. You're different.'

'I haven't got financial security, only what I earn.'

'Exactly, but it doesn't worry you, does it? To you, there are other things in life. There aren't—for Yvonne. Money is the beginning and end of everything. As soon as she heard about the castle, she started planning how to make it earn money.'

'Was it Yvonne who persuaded you to go to the solicitor?'

Peter laughed. 'In a way. She nagged like mad and of course I ignored it. Then it struck me that I owed it to Dad to look after it. Then, as you know, I met you and changed my mind.'

'Then that article was published and you changed your mind again,' Cindy put in. 'I wish I knew who phoned the newspaper. I didn't.' She looked up at him angrily. 'You think I'm a liar, but I'm not,' she said, and began to run down the slope.

'Watch out!' Peter shouted, chasing after her, catching up, grabbing her hand and running with her.

As she ran, Cindy looked straight ahead. She was afraid if she turned to look at him, he might see the truth in her eyes. Why must she love this man? she asked herself miserably. If only it was possible to control love! If only . . .

They were both a little breathless as they reached the castle. The sun shining on it seemed to increase its majesty—some of the trees had a few green buds and the snowdrops were pushing their way bravely through the cold soil as usual.

'Spring won't be long,' Cindy said gaily.

'Spring comes late here,' Peter began.

'Do you have to be so depressing?' Cindy asked laughing.

'I'm a realist, not a dreamer like you.'

'Remember what you said that day? Something about a golden maze,' Cindy asked as they went inside the castle.

'Peter!' Yvonne came storming down the hall, her cheeks bright red, her eyes flashing. 'You must speak to that impossible creature, Paul Stone. Impudent! I've never heard such cheek in all my life or such bad language—and I thought I'd heard most. There he was—down in one of the vaults, digging. What are you doing? I asked. He told me to mind my own business and I said it was my business, and then he was rude and said it had no right to be my business . . .' She stopped, glaring at Peter, who was laughing. 'I don't see anything funny in that.' She turned to Cindy. 'Do you?'

'No, I don't,' Cindy agreed.

Peter stopped laughing. 'Sorry, Yvonne, but you get so involved with the word *business* I couldn't help laughing. That young man has got to pull up his socks. He's been able to do just what he likes too long. Why was he digging?'

'He wouldn't tell me.'

Mrs. Stone appeared, banging the gong. She, too, looked angry.

'I'm hungry, aren't you, Cindy?' Peter asked, leading the way. 'Walking gives one an appetite.'

Yvonne sulked all through lunch, hardly saying a word. Cindy felt uncomfortable, particularly as Peter was obviously finding it hard not to laugh, but as they drank coffee, Peter said:

'Cheer up, Yvonne, it isn't the end of the world. I'll speak to Stone.'

Her face changed. 'You will? And find out why he was digging, Peter. That's most important. You won't forget, will you?'

'No, I won't forget,' he promised.

It amazed Cindy, but Yvonne's whole attitude changed. She turned to Cindy and began to talk in a friendly voice, asking questions about her work, and it was only as they finished their coffee that she turned to Peter again and asked him in a casual voice, a voice so casual that it caught Cindy's attention:

'By the way, Peter, doesn't Claife mean a steep hillside with path? I can't find the path. There must have been one to give the castle its name. That Paul Stone knows where it is. He told me so and refused to tell me where it was.' Her voice shook angrily. 'Perhaps you know the path?'

'The path?' Peter looked puzzled. 'I never thought of there being one.'

'Oh dear, it is so annoying. Look, Peter, you find out from Stone. You're his boss. He'll have to tell you.'

Peter stood up. 'I can hardly twist his arm, can I, but I'll do my best. It's time he realised who's the boss round here. I'm afraid he's done what he likes too long.'

He left them and Cindy wondered how she could get away tactfully, Yvonne stood up and wandered round the room, then turned.

'Cindy, I wonder what would be the best colour for the curtains in here. We ought to have it centrally heated too.'

'I thought Peter wanted it to be furnished in the way it would have been in the period this castle represents.'

'Does he? We've got to consider the best way to make money, not some sentimental idea . . . We shall only live here part of the year, because London must be our headquarters. I'll have to get a good manager, for Peter is hopeless at judging characters, he's too much of a romantic.'

'A romantic?' echoed Cindy, and began to laugh.

Peter came in. 'What's the joke?' he demanded.

'Yvonne says you're a romantic, Peter.'

He gave her an odd look. 'You don't think I

116

am?'

'Most certainly not,' Cindy said firmly.

'Did you see Paul Stone?' Yvonne demanded.

'I did.'

'And what did he say?'

'Nothing. Precisely nothing,' said Peter, sounding amused.

'But, Peter, he must have said something!'

'My dear Yvonne, he did. He talked for a long time and at the end had said precisely nothing. I gather the digging in the vaults was because of the rats.'

'Rats?' Yvonne sounded worried. 'I didn't see one down there.'

'It seems they roam at night. Stone is putting down poison or something.'

'And the path?' Yvonne asked eagerly.

'He says he's heard of it, folk talk of it in the village. He doesn't know where the path exactly is, but reckons it would start from the lake but has grown over long ago.'

'I thought you said he had told you nothing?' said Cindy.

Peter smiled. 'Well, what I've just told you took an awful long time to say. A sort of intelligentsia type, using long words whose meaning he probably doesn't know himself. Anyhow, I made it clear that he mustn't be rude to you—he said you were rude to him. That he wasn't a *serf* . . . that was the word he used,' Peter sounded amused. 'Apparently you

117

were rather arrogant, Yvonne.'

'Arrogant? Me? I merely told him that he was your employee and had no right to dig in the vaults without your permission.'

Cindy, murmuring something, slipped away from the two of them and escaped to her room. Somehow their wrangling made it all much worse, for they had sounded like a couple who had been married for years and who enjoyed a quarrel because of the fun of making it up afterwards! The more Cindy saw them together, the more convinced was she that they would one day marry, for Yvonne seemed so sure of herself, so possessive with Peter.

If only the week would end, Cindy thought miserably, and she could go miles away, never to see them again. Yet, inconsistently, the idea made her want to cry, for how *could* she say good-bye to Peter, knowing she would never see him again.

In the morning, soon after breakfast, Yvonne vanished. Peter asked Cindy if she would like to walk round the castle with him, giving him her ideas of what they should do to turn it into a profitable business.

'I'd love to,' she said, her face glowing with surprised pleasure before she had time to hide it. 'Yvonne says though that . . .'

Peter smiled. 'Let's forget Yvonne, she's full of ideas. I still prefer yours. I think a lot of people, particularly from abroad, would enjoy

118

the feeling that they were living in a replica of an old castle. We wouldn't fool them, we'd just make it as much like it would have been in the old days. I'm afraid you'll have to do a lot of research on it for me.'

Cindy caught her breath. So Peter was not going to walk out of her life? Or perhaps it would be more accurate to say he was not going to let her walk out of his.

'I'll enjoy it,' she said breathlessly.

They took their time, wandering up and down the different flights of stairs, going into the lofty cold rooms, many of them filled with furniture that was covered with sacking.

'When Mother was alive, everything was different,' Peter said wistfully.

'I imagine in those days you had quite a big staff?'

'Actually we did. I suppose Dad, on his own, didn't need them. I wonder why he took on Mrs. Stone?'

'Ask Mrs. Usher,' Cindy suggested. 'She knows everything.'

Peter laughed, 'I will, too!'

They went down into the vaults. No sign of Paul Stone anywhere. It was dark and cold and Cindy shivered, imagining the days long gone by when in real castles these horrible places might be full of prisoners.

'I wonder where Yvonne is?' she said as they went back to what Peter called the civilised part and Mrs. Stone brought them

119

coffee.

Peter gave Cindy an odd look. 'She's a perfectionist. She has some idea that the imaginary path—for that's what I think it is— holds some secret and that it must be discovered if we're to get the castle's full value.' He laughed. 'Honestly, Cindy, she amazes me. That girl has a one-track mind: money! She can't bear to be cheated or fooled.'

Cindy sat silently, listening as Peter tried to make her *understand* Yvonne. He did it in a surprisingly gentle way, almost as if he was a father, talking of a difficult child he loved. For it seemed to Cindy that Peter's love for Yvonne showed all the way through.

Yvonne joined them just before lunch. She looked tired and bad-tempered.

'You'd think some of the locals would know about the path,' she grumbled. 'Or is it just that they won't tell me?'

'Why not go and ask Mrs. Usher?' Cindy suggested. 'She's very helpful.'

'Where does she live?' Yvonne asked, so Cindy told her. 'I'll go down this afternoon.'

'Mrs. Usher likes an after-lunch nap, Yvonne,' Peter pointed out.

Yvonne frowned. 'So what?'

'Why not go about half past three?' said Cindy. 'She'll give you a marvellous tea.'

Cindy went walking that afternoon, but first she drove down to the village and parked her car before walking along the side of the lake. Here she was under the shadow of the mountain behind her, but she could just see the castle through the groups of trees. It was cold and she shivered, but anything was better than staying in the castle and listening to Yvonne laying down the law as to what should be done to make the castle a financial success. Peter must really love her, Cindy thought, to have the patience to listen to her all the time. It was odd, because Peter was *not* a patient man. Nor was he . . . what was the word . . . biddable. He did what he liked. Yet he often seemed to give way to Yvonne. It could only mean one thing: he loved her.

That evening, the guests arrived for dinner: Luke and Maidie Fairhead, Mrs. Usher, David Baxter and Johanna Younge. Mrs. Stone cooked a delicious dinner of roast duckling and the conversation was easygoing. Cindy sat next to Luke Fairhead with David on her other side. David hardly spoke to her, but that didn't matter, for Luke Fairhead had plenty to say. Yvonne, of course, was very much the hostess, but afterwards as they all went to the drawing-room to have coffee round the huge log fire, David Baxter went to sit by Yvonne, Cindy by Mrs. Usher, and Johanna was left with the Fairheads and Peter.

Not unnaturally both the Fairheads had a lot of questions to ask Peter, for both were interested in his adventures since he left.

Johanna sat still, looking attractive, her hands folded almost meekly as she looked at Peter, but Cindy noticed that she kept glancing to where David and Yvonne were talking seriously.

Poor Johanna, Cindy thought, loving David, and now Yvonne has walked in, for despite Johanna's beauty, she was nothing in comparison with Yvonne, who was years younger and much more beautiful. Cindy sighed, glad she had Mrs. Usher to talk to, for Cindy knew she was the plainest of them all.

'It must be wonderful to be so beautiful,' she said wistfully to Mrs. Usher.

The little old lady chuckled. 'They pay a price later. Can you imagine how ghastly it must be to look in the mirror and say: "My, can that be me?" in horror?'

Cindy laughed, 'I say that all the time!'

Mrs. Usher looked at her. 'Your trouble, child, is that you believed what those naughty cousins of yours said. You mustn't. Can't you see they wouldn't have said it if they weren't jealous?'

Cindy was startled. 'They were jealous of me?'

'Why not? Your face has an unusual charm, a sort of fey look. Heart-shaped, with huge dark eyes and the prettiest of hair. You look kind of cute with your glasses on.'

'Oh, Mrs. Usher, that's just what Mr. Jenkins—he's my boss—said.'

'Did he now? Shows the man had some sense. Tell me what he said.'

It was quite early when Johanna said she must go. Peter took her to her car and when he came back he had a puzzled look, Cindy noticed.

Gradually everyone went, the last being David, who seemed unwilling to leave.

'That'll be fun. David,' Yvonne said gaily. 'I'll meet you for lunch tomorrow. Peter will drive me in.'

As Cindy went to her room, she realised with a shock that her week was nearly up. On Sunday she could go back to London. How swiftly the last few days had gone. The best was would be to slip off early on Sunday, before breakfast perhaps, leaving the diary and a letter for Peter. No doubt they'd be glad to go down and find she had gone—for good.

But the diary must be somewhere safe. Cindy thought worriedly; whatever happened, Peter must see it. Maybe it would be safer if she took it back to London and then posted it to him? If she registered it, he'd have to get it, because it could be traced.

At breakfast next morning, Peter looked at Cindy.

'Yvonne's lunching with my cousin. Care to come along and we can lunch somewhere? Good idea? Looks as if it's going to be a nice day after all.'

Yvonne buttered her toast and looked up.

123

'You don't mind me lunching with David, Peter?'

He looked surprised. 'Of course not, Yvonne. I'm afraid we never got on well.'

'So I gathered. I wonder why? He seems intelligent, easy to talk to, full of good ideas.'

'That invariably fail and he rushes to someone with a soft heart for help. I gather from Luke that David practically bled Dad, always asking for money.'

'Oh, Mr. Fairhead!' Yvonne said scornfully. 'These narrow-minded country people! No doubt your father saw David as the son who'd let him down.'

A dull flush filled Peter's cheeks and Cindy wondered what he'd say. To her surprise he merely smiled:

'Is that David's line? Well, I've some work to do, but I'll pick you both up round about twelve. Okay?'

'Okay,' they agreed, and he left them.

Yvonne glanced at Cindy. 'You don't like David?'

'I don't know him. I did think he was—well, very unlike Peter when I could really see him.'

'It must be an awful bind having to wear glasses,' Yvonne said sympathetically. 'It makes you lose all your real personality.'

Cindy managed a laugh. 'I loathed them when I was younger, but I'm beginning to get used to them. My boss told me that I was even prettier in them.'

Yvonne laughed. 'Some boss! He likes you, I take it.'

'Actually he's very sweet. None of the other girls can stand him, because he loses his temper and shouts at them.'

'And not at you?' Yvonne poured herself out some more coffee.

'Oh yes, he yells at me more than at them, but I know he doesn't mean it. You see, he can never forgive himself if he makes a mistake. And he makes lots, so he has to yell at someone who happens to be handy.'

'It sounds as though you're in love with him,' commented Yvonne. 'Rather surprises me, because I thought . . .'

Peter came into the room. 'Yvonne, David's on the phone and wants to speak to you.'

'Oh no! I hope he doesn't want to cancel our lunch, because I've a lot of questions to ask him. I was wondering if a boutique would pay off in Keswick.'

'I think there are several already,' Peter said drily.

'That means there's a market.' Yvonne gulped down the remains of her coffee and hurried from the room.

Peter stayed, leaning against the door. 'What were you two talking about?' he asked.

Cindy hastily finished her coffee, too. 'About my boss.'

'Are you in love with him?'

Cindy hesitated. Maybe she should pretend

she was and then Peter could never guess the truth.

'Well, not really,' she said slowly. 'I do like him very much. He's thoughtful and kind.'

'These are important traits to you?'

'Traits?' Cindy wrinkled her face as she tried to understand and then she nodded, her hair swinging. 'Oh yes. I think one wants to be loved by someone kind.'

'He loves you? He's said so?'

'Oh no, of course not,' Cindy said hastily. 'There's never been any question. I mean, I don't really know him.'

'He's never taken you out to lunch?' Peter said drily.

'Lunch? Goodness, no! Oh, once he did take me out to dinner, but that was different.'

'Why was it different?' Peter came and straddled a chair, looking at her curiously.

'Well, we'd been working very late. He'd been away ill and everything had just piled up. There was just Mr. Jenkins and me in the office and we both had a shock when we saw the time. It was nine-thirty! "I'm starving" he said, "so must you be, let's get something to eat."' Cindy laughed. 'We were both so tired he yawned all through the meal, and then he paid for a taxi to take me home.'

'Home?'

'I have a bed-sitter in Earls Court.'

'Did you ask him in for a drink?'

Cindy looked startled. 'Of course not! I

could hardly stay awake. Besides, he didn't come with me, just put me in the taxi and gave me a pound note. He said I could give him the change next day—which I did.'

'Very thoughtful of him. I expect he'll be glad you're going back.'

Cindy laughed. 'He told me I mustn't stay away more than a week or he'd go mad. None of the other girls can stand him, nor he them. He says they can't spell and the files get in a mess.'

'And you can spell and the files don't get in a mess?' Peter asked, a strange smile on his face.

'Yes, I am lucky that way,' Cindy said gravely. 'It's just having a photographic memory.'

'Useful.' Peter looked at his watch. 'I must go. I want a talk with Johanna Younge. She was very strange last night when I saw her out to her car. She said she was sure she'd seen Yvonne before, yet she couldn't place her. Then she said she might remember it in the night and would I look in to see her.' He laughed. 'She's very amusing as a rule, but I don't know what was wrong last night, because I've never known her so quiet. Not that I ever really *knew* her. I think we actually met once, but she used to go to the Club quite a lot and I saw her there, the life and soul of the party. Last night she was very . . . well, not herself.'

Cindy hesitated. Should she tell him that

127

Johanna was in love with David and that he'd had eyes only for Yvonne? Peter was in one of his gentle moods, but was just as likely to change, and he might accuse her of being unkind to Yvonne, so Cindy decided to say nothing.

Peter drove them to Kendal where Yvonne was meeting David and then he drove Cindy around. The sun shone, the snow on top of the mountains sparkled, the lakes looked placid, the villages were huddled together. Together they admired Windermere with the distant mountains and the trees sheltering the little stone houses.

'I imagine that lake would be packed in the summer,' Peter said drily. 'Steamers and launches.'

They went to Thirlmere, to Derwentwater, finally lunching at Keswick. Cindy had been quiet all the way; indeed she had little chance to talk, for Peter seemed full of life and kept her amused with tales of the first time he went climbing, and how once when camping he had crawled into his sleeping bag to find it full of water. He really seemed cheerful and she was glad, for it meant she would have a happy memory of this, their last day together.

At lunch he startled her by saying abruptly:

'I expect you're looking forward to being back at work on Monday.'

'Well, I . . .' Cindy wasn't sure what to say.

'You must have missed your friends and

128

found life rather boring up here as well as lonely.'

Cindy stared at him in amazement. All those things were the very last she could have felt up here. Everything had happened so fast, so much had happened.

'I've . . . I've thoroughly enjoyed my stay here. I certainly wasn't bored.'

'Good. Only it's a drab life for the very young.'

'I'm not the very young,' she said slowly.

He laughed and she saw he was teasing her and she had, as usual, risen to the bait.

'Anyhow, your boss'll be glad to have you back,' Peter said cheerfully, as if that finalised everything.

Afterwards he drove her round the lakes again, showing her what they had missed. He showed her the Langdale Pikes, even taking her to the Dungeon Ghyll Force where the waterfall plunges sixty feet into a basin-like valley between huge cliffs. At Blea Tarn, they looked back at Great Langdale. It was all so beautiful, even though parts of the bleak mountains were eerily depressing, and this would be her last view for she knew that she would never come up here again. Once she had gone out of Peter's life, she must never return. That was the only way to avoid heartache . . . if it was to be avoided, which she doubted.

Finally they drove back to the castle.

129

'Enjoy the trip?' Peter asked her cheerfully.

'Very much,' Cindy said brightly. It meant nothing to him at all that she was going away, nothing whatsoever. He had met her and now she was going. It was as simple as that.

In any case, why should he miss her when he had Yvonne to be his companion?

Yvonne looked up to greet them. She was sitting at the table, papers before her and a pen in her hand.

'I've got a wonderful idea, Peter. David and I think it would work,' she said eagerly. 'Now if we were to build on at the back of the castle . . .'

Cindy escaped to her bedroom and reached it just in time before the tears came. She stood in the middle of the room, her hands pressed against her eyes as she tried to stop crying. The castle was Yvonne's—Yvonne's and Peter's, and it looked as if David was easing his way in and she was the one left out. This was a fact Cindy had to accept—the hardest she had ever known.

The evening seemed endless, Yvonne chatting away while Peter listened patiently and Cindy twisted her hair round her hand until Yvonne told her to stop fidgeting.

'You're not a child, Cindy. Do grow up!' she said in the patient voice of an exasperated adult.

'I'm sorry, I didn't realise.' Cindy said, and stood up. 'I think I'll have an early night.'

'Good idea!' Yvonne smiled sweetly. 'You have a long journey tomorrow.'

Both of them, though neither had mentioned it, had remembered that that day was Cindy's last. Both probably were pleased, Cindy thought miserably.

She carefully packed her clothes, putting Uncle Robert's diary under everything. The first thing she would do in London would be to post it back and register it! At least in that way she could repay Uncle Robert a little for his remembering her.

It was hard to sleep. She hugged her pillow, almost like a child hugging her teddy bear for comfort. How could she bear it? she asked herself. How could she look at Peter and calmly say 'Goodbye'?

Next morning she awoke early and she got up soon after six, washed, dressed and hastily scribbled a note for Peter.

'Thanks for everything, Cindy.'

She crept down the stairs of the quiet castle, left the note on the silver platter in the hall, and then hoping the heavy wooden door's squeaks and groans wouldn't wake someone up, she let herself outside, her suitcase in hand.

Quickly she walked round the back to the garages. As she backed the car out, Paul Stone walked out of the kitchen.

'Where are you off to?' he asked.

'Home,' she said simply, and drove away.

131

It was still very dark, the sky starting to brighten, and Cindy drove carefully along the track back towards the main road, but suddenly it began to rain. It was only a drizzle, but it blotted out the fells and now the depressing mistiness came down to shut out the new light and everything else. Cindy felt a strangely frightening feeling of finality— almost as if she was in a small oasis of isolation. Again she felt the terrible depression she had known before she heard of her chance to own the castle—the awful feeling of belonging to no one, of knowing that no one cared about her.

She had to drive slowly, for it was difficult to see, but as she reached the main road, the mist lifted and everything was for a brief moment beautifully clear. Then the rain fell and really fell. A great grey curtain of water was before her and her windscreen wipers seemed inadequate to do their job. Suddenly the car skidded and though she tried to save it, went off the road, bouncing against a tree and stopping dead.

For a moment she sat stunned. Luckily she had been crawling along, so she had not been flung forward through the windscreen, only bumping her head badly. She moved her legs, arms and hands nervously. Nothing was broken!

She heard a car draw up and someone shouting and turned as a man came running towards her. Dimly she saw his face, but did not know him, and then everything went black . . .

When she came round something hot was stinging her throat and she opened her eyes to see the man bending over her, a flask at her mouth as he gently eased down a little brandy.

'Nasty shock,' he said tersely. 'Skidded, eh? Lucky thing you were going so slowly. I was behind you. Could hardly see a thing.'

'It . . . it was a bit of a shock,' Cindy whispered. 'I . . . I think I'm all right.'

'But your car isn't. We'll have to get it towed. I'm taking you to a hospital.'

'But I'm all right,' Cindy said quickly.

'Is that so?' he asked, amused. He was a man of about Luke Fairhead's age, Cindy saw. 'You should see the bulge on your head! Reckon by tomorrow your eyes will be black. No, I'm taking you along to have an X-ray. Can't be too careful about bumps on the head. Come along, see if you can walk to my car. I'll bring your suitcase and lock your car, then I'll phone a garage for you.'

Cindy managed to get out of the car. Her legs felt absurdly shaky and yet she felt quite well.

'Where were you off to?' he asked as he helped her walk along slowly.

'London. I've got to go . . . I must be at work tomorrow.'

The man chuckled. 'A likely story! You can

133

ring your boss and explain. Reckon he wouldn't want you around with two black eyes. You been on holiday?'

'I've been staying . . . staying at Claife Castle.'

'Oh, there,' the man laughed. 'It's certainly been in the news lately. You must be Miss Preston.'

'Yes.' A spurt of energy filled Cindy. 'And I did *not* promise to sell the castle to any American!' she said angrily.

'Of course you didn't,' the man said soothingly, helping her into his car. 'If you'd promised, you'd not have been such a fool as to tell the world, now would you?'

Cindy hadn't thought of it from that angle. She wondered why Peter hadn't.

The man hurried and got the suitcase which he put in the boot, then handed her the car keys.

'This is very good of you, Mr . . .?' said Cindy. She was beginning to feel better. Gently she touched her forehead. He was right, there was a swelling there.

'Eastwood. Tony Eastwood. A married man with six children, five girls and a boy,' he said cheerfully. 'Now I'm taking you to the hospital for an X-ray.'

'I don't think . . .'

He turned and smiled. Now she could see that he was a big man with a double chin and dark eyes and practically bald. She put her hand to her glasses. How easily she could have broken them!

'Your nose is a bit cut,' he told her with a grin. 'Don't think your beauty will be harmed.'

'My beauty?' Cindy found herself laughing. 'This is good of you!'

'Pleasure. Think what a wonderful dinner-story this will be. By the way, I gather the real heir turned up, so the castle isn't yours? Bad luck. A rare old monstrosity, but you can't help being fond of it. What'll the real heir do? Sell it?'

'Oh no, he's got lots of plans . . .' Cindy stopped abruptly. After all, she didn't know the truth. She had no idea just what Peter's future plans would be. Would he follow her suggestion and make it into a mock-medieval castle, or Yvonne's and turn it into an up-to-date hotel?

They stopped outside a long building and Mr. Eastwood took Cindy in, handing her over to the casualty doctor.

'I'll come back for you,' he promised. 'Meanwhile I'll arrange for your car to be towed to a garage.'

'Will it take long? The repairs, I mean,' Cindy asked worriedly.

'Not more than a few days, I reckon.'

'A few days?' Cindy caught her breath with dismay. 'Then I'd better stay at a hotel near the garage . . .'

'Don't you worry, just leave it all to me,' Mr.

135

Eastwood said, striding away, leaving Cindy sitting in the chair, waiting for her X-ray.

CHAPTER TEN

Cindy had just been told that the X-ray showed no damage had been done when a little nurse came and said:

'The gentleman is waiting outside, Miss Preston.'

Following the nurse to the square in front of the hospital, Cindy stopped still, staring unbelievingly before her.

'It's you!' she gasped.

Peter came forward with a grin. 'Who else? I've got your suitcase in the car.'

'But, Peter, I asked Mr. Eastwood to find me a hotel while the car's repaired.'

'Mr. Eastwood had enough sense to know I wouldn't allow that. You're coming back to the castle with me and going to bed. It must have been quite a shock.' He gripped her arm firmly and led her to the car. 'He told me you were driving very carefully or it could have been what he called a nasty business.'

'But, Peter, I've got to get to London and ...'

'You can phone your boss. I'm sure a kind man will understand,' he said sarcastically.

Cindy looked at him quickly. 'I'd really rather not come back.'

'I'm afraid you have no choice,' he said casually. 'As I said once before, I'm much bigger and stronger than you.'

'Oh, Peter . . .' Cindy began, and then, just as before, found herself laughing. 'What do you propose to do? Drag me by my hair?'

He glanced at her as he drove through the High Street, past the impressive Cross in the middle of the road.

'Well, it's long enough. The X-ray was okay?'

'Yes, nothing's wrong with me.'

'Good. The car won't take long. Probably be ready by Wednesday.'

'Wednesday?' Cindy almost wailed.

'Your boss can always cut it out of your holiday time if he feels like it.'

'He wouldn't!'

'Of course not. I was forgetting what a fine man he is,' Peter said, again in an odd voice which made Cindy glance at him. 'Why did you go off without saying goodbye, Cindy?'

'I left a note. I hate goodbyes.'

'As it turned out, it wasn't.'

She wondered what Yvonne would say and wasn't at all surprised when they reached the castle to have Yvonne look at her and say:

'I might have known it! You castle maniacs just can't stay away. It's in your blood like some virus.'

'I hardly think Cindy's so addicted to the castle as to risk her life,' Peter said drily, for which Cindy was grateful.

She went to bed—not because she felt ill but because she felt exhausted, limp, unable to face up to Yvonne's accusing eyes or Mrs. Stone's disapproving face. On Monday she stayed in bed, too, pleading nervous exhaustion and no doubt pleasing both Yvonne and Peter, she thought. He had sent up quite a few books for her to read from the library, so she was quite happy—except now and then when she realised Peter was downstairs and that she was deliberately denying herself the pleasure of his company. But was it pleasure, she wondered, when it hurt so much? Her eyes were black as her rescuer had expected.

Next day Cindy decided she couldn't pretend any longer to be ill, so she went down for breakfast.

'Had a good rest?' Yvonne greeted her. 'My word, your eyes!'

Cindy smiled. 'I feel fine, thanks. I must phone my boss. Is that okay, Peter?'

'Of course, be my guest,' he said.

'Isn't that what she is?' Yvonne asked sweetly.

'Not a very willing one,' Peter said with a chuckle. 'I had to practically force her to come back.'

Yvonne looked sceptical.

'How long will the car be, did you say, Peter?' Cindy asked. 'I could go up by train . . .'

'That's absurd. You'd have to come back to fetch the car. I think it'll be ready tomorrow or

139

the next day.'

'Then I *could* be back at work on Thursday . . .'

'Depends on the weather. If the fog comes down, better make it the following Monday,' Peter said with a grin.

The telephone was in the library, so after ten o'clock, remembering her boss's late appearance at the office, Cindy phoned him.

'You've what?' he said. 'Had a car accident? Are you all right?'

'I'm fine. I had to have an X-ray as I hit my head, but everything's okay. It's the car. It got rather badly damaged and may take a few days to be put right. You do understand? Oh, thanks so much, I knew you would. Thank you very much indeed. That's lovely,' Cindy finished warmly, and replaced the receiver.

Peter stood in the doorway, an odd look on his face.

'He took it all right?'

'Oh yes,' Cindy smiled. 'He was quite worried. Told me to rest, as delayed shock often happens days later. He says I'm not to go back to work until next Monday . . . but all the same, Peter, I'd like to go as soon as the car is ready.'

'Of course, I understand your eagerness to return to your job,' he said curtly, and walked out of the room.

The next thing was to write to Keith Ayres. Not that there was much to say, just that now

Peter, the real heir, had turned up, she was leaving as soon as she could.

'I expect you saw the article in the paper,' she wrote. 'I imagine it had something to do with the letter I posted you. No one here—or at least only a couple—will believe me when I say I didn't phone the newspaper, in fact didn't know *anything* about the American's offer. It hasn't been very nice for me, being practically called a liar, and I shall be glad to be back in London. It was maddening to have the accident just as I was on my way back. I'm all right, but the car needs repairing and I don't think I'll be back much before Thursday or Friday.'

She sealed the envelope and drove down to the village, borrowing Peter's car. Not eager to get back to the castle, she went into Johanna's tea-shop.

Johanna came to greet her. 'Nice to see you. Sure you're all right? Your poor eyes!'

'You heard about the accident,' Cindy pretended to sigh. 'One can't do anything in this village without everyone knowing.'

Bringing two cups of coffee, Johanna sat down opposite Cindy.

'She's very beautiful,' Johanna said abruptly.

Cindy looked at her sympathetically. 'I know.'

'I hear she had lunch with David next day?'
'Yes.'

There was a silence while they both looked at one another. 'I thought it was her and Peter,' said Johanna.

'I still think so,' Cindy told her quickly, and saw the relief in Johanna's eyes. 'I think she was talking business with David. Something about opening a boutique up here.'

'Is that all?' Johanna seemed to relax. 'You know, it's a funny thing, Cindy, but I'm sure I've met her somewhere. I can't place it, and yet I have this strange feeling. Maybe it's her voice. I don't know, I just don't know. I told Peter so.'

'And what did he say?'

'He looked amused and said he doubted it very much. That this was Yvonne's first trip to Cumberland and he doubted if she'd be likely to have a double.'

Cindy laughed, 'I'd doubt it, too!'

'And yet I feel certain I've met her somewhere,' Johanna mused.

Back at the castle, Cindy saw it was time for lunch, but only Peter was there. He looked puzzled.

'I thought Yvonne was with you,' he said, almost accusingly. 'I've been with Luke Fairhead all the time.'

'She wasn't with me.'

Peter shrugged. 'Maybe she's gone to see David.'

'But how could she without a car?'

'That's a point . . . or he could have called

142

for her. Mrs. Stone,' he asked as the tall thin woman brought in the plates of tomato soup, 'any idea where Miss Todd is? Did she ask Paul to drive her anywhere?'

Mrs. Stone looked quite offended. 'She did not. I saw her go off wandering down the slope—beyond t'end of the garden.'

'What would she be doing there?'

Showing off her sharp teeth, in a grimace, Mrs. Stone shrugged.

'Maybe looking for that path she's so interested in.'

'Well, we'll have lunch, but keep something hot for her, will you?' Peter asked. 'She'll probably turn up soon.'

But Yvonne didn't. At three o'clock when there was still no sign of her, Peter went in search of Cindy.

'We're going to look for her. You stay here, Cindy. I'll take Paul and Luke.'

'I'll come too,' Cindy said quickly.

'No, you won't.'

'Yes, I will,' Cindy said firmly. 'She might have fallen and hurt herself, so I'll bring some brandy.'

'Look, you'll be nothing but a nuisance . . .' Pete began, when there was a hammering at the front door.

It was Luke Fairhead and Paul Stone.

Luke spoke first. 'Ah, good, Miss Preston. You come with me and we'll drive down to the lake and start from there. Peter, you and young Stone start from the top and work your way down . . .'

'I'm going to help Mr. Fairhead, Peter,' she said firmly.

'Okay. Not so dangerous working your way up,' he said abruptly. 'Come on, Stone.'

Mr. Fairhead drove Cindy down to the lake's edge.

'I can't think what Yvonne could be doing down *here*. She's looking for that mystery path, but . . .'

Mr. Fairhead chuckled. 'Women are queer cattle, Miss Preston. I gather she's always searching for some way or other to make money.'

'I suppose money is important.'

'It's a great help when you're very young or very old. However, 'twould not be so important to me as work I love. You got a job you like?'

'I'm a secretary to a very nice man.'

'That's good. Look, we'll park this way along here now. There are some caves just above this spear of land.'

'Caves?'

'Yes, mostly grown over by grass and dangerous. Only a fool would go into them,' he said, giving her a hand as they went up the steep grass-covered side of the mountain.

They reached a small flat surface. Tall grass and matted fern covered the outside of the caves.

144

'Miss Todd!' he shouted, holding his hands over his mouth to form a funnel. 'Miss Todd!'

A faint sound replied and he turned to look at Cindy.

'I think we've found her already. You wait here,' he ordered, and broke down some of the long bracken. 'I'm coming . . .' he shouted. Then he vanished into the dark opening of the cave.

Cindy waited. All was still. She wondered if she should follow him into the cave, but then, if he didn't come out, who would there be to tell Peter? She decided to wait as Mr. Fairhead had said.

Then she heard shouts from above and she made out Peter's tall body leaning over a boulder and looking down.

'We think we've found her . . . in the caves!' Cindy shouted.

'Tell Luke to stay out. He's too fat!' Peter yelled back. But it was too late!

It was five or more minutes before Peter and Paul Stone slid to the ground by her side. Paul, grumbling under his breath, dived into the cave. Peter looked at Cindy.

'Give me your word you won't go in?' he said curtly.

Something seemed to snap inside her. 'What's the good, when you think me a liar?'

His hands closed on her arms and he shook her. 'Look, cut out this childish nonsense. I do *not* think you're a liar. If you go in there . . .

145

Look . . .' he began again. 'It can be pretty dicey in these caves. If none of us get out you'll have to call for help. If you're in as well, no one will know. Is that clear?'

'Yes, that's clear. I give you my word,' she said. 'But, Peter . . .' her voice shook a little, 'be careful, won't you?'

He gave her a strange look. 'Of course I will.'

Then he let go of her and pushed his way through the bracken into the cave. Cindy stood trembling. Three men and Yvonne in there. Why were they so long? Surely the caves weren't so big . . .

And then Luke Fairhead came out, scrambling on his knees. He stood up, brushing down his corduroy breeches and smiling at her.

'It's all right. She was caught in a narrow turn. Silly young fool, she shoulda known better.'

'Peter . . . ?' Cindy asked.

'He's coming. He and Paul are easing her along. Seems she's a bit hysterical-like. Not that I blame her. Fair gives you a fright, stuck in those dark caves.'

'Why did she go in there in the first place?' Cindy asked.

A question that Peter repeated an hour later after they had carried Yvonne to the car, driven her back to the castle and got her propped up in a chair, sipping some brandy.

146

'Why on earth did you go in alone, Yvonne?' he asked angrily, impatiently pacing up and down. 'Any fool knows these caves aren't safe.'

'Well, this fool didn't,' said Yvonne. She was apparently over her shock and fear. 'I find caves fascinating and when I saw this big cave with the high roof, I thought I could squeeze round the corner. I was too fat . . .' She looked at her watch. 'You left it pretty late, Peter,' she said accusingly. 'Why didn't you come and look for me before?'

'Hadn't a clue where you were. I thought you might have sneaked off for lunch with David,' he grinned. 'Then Mrs. Stone told me you'd gone for a walk down the garden and I thought maybe you'd got down to the lake, decided to have lunch there.'

'A fine story!' Yvonne's eyes were angry. 'I suppose the truth is you just couldn't be bothered.'

'Why should I be bothered, Yvonne? You're not a child. I credited you with enough sense not to do such a crazy idiotic thing. What were you looking for in those caves?'

Yvonne looked startled. 'Looking for . . . .? Why . . . well, nothing really. I just find caves fascinating and . . .'

Cindy slipped out of the room, unnoticed. Obviously they were about to start another of their friendly 'quarrels' and she wanted to have nothing to do with it.

At dinner, the quarrel seemed to have been over and forgotten, for when Cindy joined them in the drawing-room for a drink, Peter was telling Yvonne about the castle. He looked up with a smile when Cindy arrived.

'You might be interested in this, too, Cindy,' he said as he went to pour her out a drink. 'Yvonne asked me when and why the castle was built.' He gave Cindy the glass and sat down by the huge log fire. 'It was some time in the eighteenth century that a man called Penn lived in the village. He was a farmer and through clever breeding and a stroke of luck, his sheep were exceptionally good and bought by people from overseas who were building up their farmlands. He did well and fell in love with a girl of a good family who also happened to be wealthy. Penn felt ashamed, for he had so little to offer her save money, so he had the castle built, copying some famous castle— which one, I've no idea. He hoped it would make the world treat him as an aristocrat. I don't know if it worked. Anyhow, years later a Penn married a Baxter, and that's how *we* got here. Actually Caterina—a local gipsy, you'll probably see—she tells fortunes!—she has it that the castle is cursed because its women have been so *timid*. The Mrs. Penn I was talking about is said to have been timid as a mouse and so was the Penn daughter who married a Baxter.' He gave a little grunt. 'So was my mother, another quiet little mouse.'

148

Yvonne laughed. 'Would you like a quiet little mouse for a wife, Peter?'

'Most certainly not,' he said, getting up to refill the glasses. 'It would be intolerably boring.'

Cindy looked at Yvonne, who smiled at her. Yvonne looked pleased with herself, Cindy thought. One thing, when Peter married Yvonne, he would not be married to a *quiet little mouse*, so perhaps the legend of the family curse would end?

When Cindy woke up next day, she was amazed at the rain which was coming down heavily. The clouds seemed to have split and it was hard to see the lake even as the mist curdled and then cleared for a moment before shutting out the view again. She dressed quickly and hurried downstairs. It was the same on every side. The dales looked black as tar and the whipping wind was tossing the peaceful lake, forcing the water up in the air in waves. She was glad to see Mrs. Stone had lit fires in both the dining-room and drawing-room, for it was bitterly cold.

Yvonne was irritable. 'It would rain now, just when I'm getting somewhere!'

Peter looked interested. 'Somewhere?'

'Yes, this mysterious path that no one seems to know about or where it is. It must be somewhere and I'm determined to find it. How long will the rain last?'

'Ask me!' Peter laughed. 'It can go on for

149

days or weeks.' He smiled at Cindy. 'Don't look so depressed, I don't think it will. Anyhow I have a lot to discuss with Luke, so see you both at lunch time. Don't go doing too much either of you, because I don't want two invalids on my hands.' He smiled and left them.

'Men!' Yvonne said with a sigh. 'They treat everything so casually. If they succeed, well, it's their good luck, and if they fail, it most certainly isn't their fault. A woman attacks a problem quite differently. Don't you agree, Cindy?'

'I honestly don't know. Well, yes, in a way I do agree,' Cindy said, remembering how hard she had worked at school and then at shorthand and typing so that she could escape from her unfriendly family.

'Good. We see eye to eye about a lot of things, Cindy, don't we?' Yvonne's smile was so sweet that Cindy felt nervous. Now what was Yvonne planning? It seemed it was nothing, for Yvonne merely announced that she had letters to write and would be in the library if anyone came to see her.

That could only be David Baxter, Cindy thought, as she curled up on the rug before the log fire and read the newspapers. She was leaning against an armchair and must have dozed off, for she awakened suddenly to a loud voice.

'I said get out and I mean get out! We don't take tramps in here!'

It could only be Mrs. Stone, Cindy thought at once, and scrambled to her feet. Maybe she needed help.

In the hall, Cindy stopped with surprise. It was no tramp that stood on the doorstep, asking to come in. Two walkers stood there, wearing thick dark blue trousers, bright red anoraks with matching woollen caps and colossal packs on their backs. They were dripping with water and both had long hair that hung over their faces so that you could hardly see their eyes.

'Just to get dry, please,' the girl begged, almost in tears.

'You heard what I said, we don't take in tramps any time.'

Cindy walked towards the door. 'Mrs. Stone, I'm sure Mr. Baxter wouldn't want you to turn them away. Please come in. You poor things, you certainly are wet!'

Mrs. Stone was white with fury. 'You've no right . . . just you wait!' she mumbled the words, but Cindy gathered that she was furious. Then Mrs. Stone said loudly, her shrill voice echoing in the lofty hall, 'All that water on my polished floor! In any case, we don't want no hippies any time.'

The two of them were sliding the huge bundles off their backs and taking off their wet anoraks, shaking the water off them.

They ignored Mrs. Stone and turned to Cindy.

'It began to rain just after we started walking. We didn't think it would be much. I'm Martin Haynes, and this is Roxanna Webster.'

'I'm Cindy Preston.'

Now she could see they were both about her age. Martin might even be younger in his bright yellow shirt and thick white sweater as he tossed back his long brown hair. Roxanna had long black hair that she swept back with a dramatic gesture to smile at Cindy.

'You've saved our lives. I don't think I could have walked another step!'

'Nonsense, Roxanna,' Martin said with a smile.

Cindy turned to the tall silent angry woman by her side.

'Would you please make some hot chocolate for us all, Mrs. Stone, then could you dry their clothes in the kitchen? Would you take off your boots too?' Cindy asked the two walkers. 'Then come and sit by the fire. You'll soon dry.'

Mrs. Stone's mouth was like a tightly-closed purse, but she did what Cindy asked, carried the wet clothes and boots to the kitchen and made them all hot chocolate. Sprawling on the rug by the roaring fire, they chatted.

'I don't know how you can enjoy walking when you have to carry everything . . . It must be a weight,' said Cindy.

'You get used to it.' Martin was warming his fingers by holding the mug in both hands.

'Must say it was pretty bad today.'

'They did warn us at the hostel, Martin,' Roxanna said gently.

He laughed. 'If we took notice of all the weather reports, we'd get nowhere. Must say I didn't think it could be so bad.'

'Where are you making for?'

Martin shrugged. 'Just anywhere. This is our favourite part of the world, especially in winter when no one's around.'

'You know this part well?' Yvonne asked.

Startled, Cindy turned round, for she hadn't heard Yvonne come in. Now Yvonne came eagerly to sit down by them.

'Yvonne, Roxanna, Martin,' Cindy quickly introduced them, and stood up. 'I'll just go and check that Mrs. Stone is drying your clothes,' she promised, and left them alone.

Mrs. Stone was stiff with fury as she let fly at Cindy.

'I have to keep the place clean, and no easy job is it any time and with them dripping water everywhere! Never did like that kind of hippy. Shouldn't wonder if 'tain't really burglars having a good look-see before breaking in!'

'If they make a mess, Mrs. Stone, I'll clear it up,' Cindy promised. 'But it's such a terrible day. Do you often get it like this?'

'Any time it comes down like so and stays for days, even weeks,' Mrs. Stone looked almost triumphant. 'How long will you be here?'

153

'Only until my car is repaired.' Cindy looked out of the kitchen window at the grey curtain of misty rain. 'Though I can't see myself driving through this sort of weather.'

Mrs. Stone was busy at the stove, stirring something. Now she looked up. 'When will she be going?' Mrs. Stone jerked her head and Cindy knew she could only mean Yvonne.

'I don't know.' Cindy hesitated, and Mrs. Stone put Cindy's thoughts into words.

'Maybe she won't ever go now?'

'Well, I honestly don't know.' Cindy wandered round the kitchen. 'You see, I don't really know either of them, Mrs. Stone. What a gorgeous smell! You really are a wonderful cook.'

Mrs. Stone sniffed. 'Have to be when you've a living to make and a son to rear. ' 'Twasn't easy when my husband died and I had a child and never'd done nothing but housework. Mr. Baxter . . . Mr. Robert Baxter, that is, he gave me this job. I knew 'twould be hard work, but I didn't mind. We had a home and . . . I thought,' she added bitterly, 'a future.'

Cindy hesitated. Should she stay and let Mrs. Stone weep on her shoulder? Or . . .

The bell above the kitchen door rang. Mrs. Stone hastily wiped her hands, pulled her apron straight.

'That front door,' she grumbled. 'Maybe life'd be easier working in a house rather than t'castle.'

Joining the others in the drawing-room, Cindy found Yvonne enthralled with what Martin was saying. He was leaning back on his hands, his long hair swinging as he talked dramatically. Roxanna stood up and went to meet Cindy.

'Do you think I could have a quick bath?' she whispered. 'I'm still frozen and I feel—well, messy.'

'Of course, come up with me.' Cindy led the way to the curving staircase. 'I know how you feel. The water is always marvellously hot.'

She could see Mrs. Stone at the door talking to a tall woman.

'It won't take more than a few moments any time.' The woman was half hidden in an enormous loose-hanging mackintosh with a purple scarf twisted round her head.

'You be off, we want no gipsies here!' Mrs. Stone snapped, and slammed the door.

Turning, she saw Cindy standing there.

'Only Caterina,' Mrs. Stone explained. 'Always wanting to tell fortunes, but we won't have nothing to do with such folk any time. Just layabouts, too lazy to work, that's what I say.' She gave Roxanna a suspicious look. 'Remember what I said, Miss Preston, now.'

'Yes, Mrs. Stone.'

'Who's she? Proper dragon!' Roxanna commented as they went up the stairs.

'Actually I'm very sorry for her,' said Cindy, leading the way to her bedroom. 'She was

155

Mr. Baxter's housekeeper for ten years and her son grew up here and somehow she thought the old man would leave the castle to the son.'

'But he didn't. Never does to count your chicks before they're hatched. My mum used to say that and I got real mad with her, but she was right, you know.'

'Do you really like all this walking?' Cindy asked curiously.

Roxanna gave her a quick smile. 'It isn't the walking . . .'

Cindy laughed. 'It's Martin?'

'It's always someone, isn't it?' Roxanna sighed. 'It's the only way I can get to be with him, but oh, how my feet hurt!'

Cindy showed her to the bathroom and went to wait in her bedroom, content that Yvonne should be keeping Martin occupied. As she sat there, Cindy read some of Uncle Robert's diary again. The items really were so sad—sometimes cheerful, but always with that wistfulness, that disappointment that things had turned out as they had, always blaming himself for a terrible mistake. In one case, he had written:

'I should have realised that Peter is like me. He has to be a person—not someone's shadow.'

How right Uncle Robert was, Cindy thought, curled up on the floor before the electric fire. Now David was much more of a

156

shadow—Peter was definitely a *person*.

The rain was still pelting down when Peter came in for lunch. He looked annoyed, but was pleasant to the 'guests'.

'Real bad luck,' he agreed. 'Where were you making for? I'll run you over this afternoon if you like.'

Roxanna's eyes glowed. 'Would you?' she said eagerly.

'Why not? In the morning the sun may be shining and you won't have wasted a day after all. Care to come, Yvonne?' he asked casually.

'No, thanks.' She smiled at him. 'I have some phone calls to make. Perhaps Cindy would like to.'

'I took that for granted,' Peter told her, and looked at Cindy and then at Roxanna. 'We won't go until tea-time, then you'll get to the hostel in time for your evening meal and bed.'

'Thanks a ton,' Roxanna said happily. She looked quickly at Cindy and away again. Cindy understood—a whole wonderful day without having to walk! What a girl will do for love, she thought sympathetically.

The rain was still pouring down as Peter drove them to the long grey hostel. Cindy was startled when Peter abruptly asked Martin:

'What was Yvonne talking to you about?'

Martin pushed back his hair. 'She's interested in folklore, so am I. I told her all the local legends and things.'

'She was interested?' Peter sounded

amused.

'Yes, particularly anything I knew about the castle. I didn't know much, because it isn't one really, is it? I mean, everyone knows it's a mock castle.'

'I agree. Yet she wanted to know all you could tell her about the castle? Was there much?'

'No, very little. The usual tales of the smuggling days. But every old house round the lakes and sea up here has those stories. Seen that old farmhouse near the coast with seven chimneys? Said to have been built by an old man so that each of his jealous daughters could have a chimney. Who'd want a chimney?' Martin chuckled. 'Anyhow, the legend is that only two of those chimneys have fireplaces and that the other chimneys were used to hide their smuggling treasures.'

'She was interested in that?'

'Very . . . even asked me where the house was, and when I told her it was for sale—well, she got real excited like.'

'I bet she did!' Peter laughed.

They stopped at the hostel which was comfortably settled at the foot of a mountain and facing the lake where the wind rippled the water into tiny patterns.

'Thanks a ton,' Roxanna said to Cindy. 'If it hadn't been for you . . .'

Cindy smiled, 'Good luck!'

Roxanna whispered in her ear, 'I just hope it

goes on raining!' and chuckled as she and Martin left, with their heavy packs, turning at the door of the hostel to wave.

Peter drove away. 'Funny, that,' he commented.

'What's funny?'

'Yvonne's interest in the house with seven chimneys. Surely she wouldn't be mug enough to believe that nonsense about smugglers' treasure? I mean, if there was any there, it would have been found years ago.'

Suddenly Cindy had an idea. She opened her mouth and then closed it again. Peter wouldn't believe her. He might even accuse her of cattiness or childishness. Yet she'd had a thought . . . perhaps that was why Yvonne was so keen to find the mysterious path that had given the castle its name, and why she was so concerned about the vaults and Paul Stone digging there. Did she think there was treasure hidden in the castle? Yet it might all be coincidences. It was best to keep quiet, Cindy decided.

'Was it really necessary,' Peter asked abruptly, 'to be quite so abrupt with Mrs. Stone?'

'Abrupt?' Cindy, jerked from her thoughts about Yvonne, turned in surprise. 'Was I abrupt?'

'She asked me who was the mistress here as she didn't know whose orders to obey. She seemed pretty mad.'

159

'I had to rescue them. It was the two . . .' Quickly she told him how Mrs. Stone had been turning them away, refusing them a chance to dry. 'They were wet through and looked half drowned. She was very rude to them.'

'I'm afraid she has an unfortunately abrupt manner,' said Peter, his voice suddenly cold. 'On the other hand, you have to draw the line somewhere. We can't give hospitality to every Tom, Dick and Harry.'

Cindy's cheeks burned. 'Under which heading do I come?'

'You know very well I didn't mean you!' he almost snapped at her. 'I agree you did right in asking them in. Only a couple of kids,' he said almost scornfully, and Cindy, remembering that Roxanna and Martin had been about her age, felt her cheeks burning still more. 'Shouldn't be out trekking alone. They could easily get lost. The girl didn't look as if she enjoyed it much.'

'She hates it.'

'Then why do it?'

Drawing a deep breath, Cindy turned to him. 'Are you men blind? She loves him, that's why she does it, and he's too . . . too selfish to see it!'

'You mean she walks these miles, gets half drowned, her feet painful, just because she loves that . . . ? She must be crazy!'

'Most females are. I suppose no man would do such a thing for a girl he loved,' Cindy said

160

bitterly. 'He'd expect her to mould her life the way he wanted it.'

'Well, that's right, isn't it?' he asked, his voice casual.

'No, it is not!' Cindy retorted angrily. 'There should be compromise. It shouldn't all be for one to have his own way.'

'But you're as bad as the rest of them, Cindy. Look how eager you are to get back to your boss, and I bet he whistles the tune, and you do what he says even when you don't like it.'

'The boss . . .' she began, and stopped. 'He never asks me to do anything I don't want to.'

Peter whistled softly. 'Well, well, well, aren't we a lucky girl!'

She clenched her hands, fighting the desire to smack his face. Instead she turned her back and looked out at the rain-drenched world. Where had the beauty of the mountains and lakes gone? The stark loveliness of the leafless trees had vanished in the mist. Now everything was grey sheets of rain and the maddening tick-tack-tick-tock of the windscreen wipers.

CHAPTER ELEVEN

It was not until they were near the castle that Peter broke the silence, and then only casually, almost as if unaware it had existed.

'Cindy, as I said, I would be grateful if you'd do some research for me about the castle. I think it was designed to be like the castles built in the eleventh and twelfth centuries, but I'm not sure as to the date. I'd like to know what sort of furniture they had in that period and the clothes, so that the staff could wear them. Wasn't it your idea in the first place? After all, as you said, in Ireland it's successful and there are quite a lot of people who'd get a kick out of living in the past, but, as I say, I want it to be the *right* background.'

Cindy turned round a little. She was tempted to refuse, yet knew she never could.

'I'll go to some of the museums and libraries. You are going to run it as a hotel?'

'I can think of no other way. It would cost the earth to have it as a mere home and it's far too big. I did think of it as a school, but can't imagine it somehow, can you?'

'No.' Cindy had to laugh, imagining the swarms of little boys or girls racing up the stairs. 'Actually I think it would be rather dangerous. They'd have to rail off the garden.'

'You're right. It's a bit too close to danger.'

'You're selling the farm?'

'Yes. I've persuaded old Colin Pritchard to come and be my head gardener. There's a cottage on the fell that he can have, so he'll be quite happy. I'm only keeping ground enough for a flower and vegetable garden and of course somewhere the guests can sit in the sun . . . I might even build a little folly—you know, those comic little sort of summerhouses they built.'

'That's a good idea,' Cindy said warmly. 'You'll want a lot of staff.'

'I thought of keeping Mrs. Stone as housekeeper, in charge of the staff. She was good to the old man and seems very efficient.'

'She is. And Paul?'

Peter frowned as he turned off the main road and they began to jolt and slide on the muddy track. 'I'm not sure. I'll have a good talk with him. He's done absolutely nothing to the garden, but he's a good driver and quite a good mechanic, so I might keep him for that.'

'You oughtn't to have cars, but coaches,' Cindy pointed out.

'Help! You're right. But can you imagine a coach going down that narrow winding road to the village?'

'Yet it must have done once.'

'You're right, you know.' Peter sounded surprised.

The rain seemed to have lessened a little as they came in sight of the castle. Cindy gave it a desperate look, she loved it so much. It seemed to her that she was always saying goodbye to it. When would she finally go?

'When will my car be ready?' she asked.

'Ready? Oh, about Thursday or Friday.'

'It's taking longer than we expected,' she said, dismayed.

Peter shrugged. 'So it seems.'

Cindy pleaded a headache as an excuse to go early to bed and after coffee in the drawing-room, left them talking. Half way upstairs, she remembered she had left her book there, so went back. As she began to open the door, she heard Peter say:

'Planning to buy a house with seven chimneys?' he asked as if amused.

'So what if I am?' Yvonne snapped back.

Cindy pulled the door to gently. Were they going to start another of those wrangles that depressed her so much? She went up to her bedroom; she would read Uncle Robert's diary instead. There were so many notes and the handwriting so small that there was still quite a lot she hadn't read yet.

It was tea time next day that Keith Ayres arrived. Peter and Yvonne were having tea with Cindy. It was a chilly, dismal day, though the rain was less severe. Yvonne was in a strange mood, hardly talking, constantly looking at Cindy as if she wanted to say something but was hesitating.

Mrs. Stone ushered him in. 'Mr. Keith

Ayres,' she announced.

He stood in the doorway staring at them. They were startled and showed it. Then he went straight to Cindy.

'Miss Preston? Good to see you again.' He turned to Peter and held out his hand. 'Mr. Baxter, I came up to settle some small details.' He looked at Yvonne and waited for Peter to introduce her, which he did promptly.

'Sit down, have a cup?' Peter asked.

'No, thank you. I had rather a big lunch on the way. I can only stay for a night and if you can't put me up, I can go to a hotel somewhere, but there are a few things we have to clear up.'

He sat down, speaking curtly as if angry. Cindy wondered why, for he had been so different before. He was a good-looking, older man, with slightly greying hair and a friendly smile when he looked at her.

'Of course you can stay here. I'll tell Mrs. Stone to get your room ready,' said Peter, leaving them.

There was a little silence. 'You are the solicitor?' Yvonne asked.

Keith Ayres looked at her. 'Yes, I am,' he said, his words clipped.

Peter returned and sat down. 'Was it a bad journey up? I mean much fog?'

'Pretty unpleasant, but it got better when I got nearer here.' He looked round. 'It's quite some place, isn't it? I'm not surprised Miss

Preston liked it.' He smiled at Cindy. Then he looked at Peter. 'I have an important thing to tell you which I believe may be of interest. You know all that hullabaloo about the American who wanted to buy this castle?' He waited until they had nodded, then he folded his arms and looked from face to face. 'Well, the whole thing was a hoax. There was no American.'

'But then . . .' Cindy began.

'No American?' Peter echoed slowly. 'Then why was it in the paper?'

Keith Ayres looked at Yvonne.

'That's absurd,' she said. 'There was a letter from him.'

'I know, Miss Preston sent it to me—unopened.' He looked at Peter thoughtfully. 'One point was rather interesting. The letter had been posted several days earlier and should have reached the castle *before* the article in the newspaper appeared. Something went wrong and the letter was delayed.'

'Paul Stone said the letter *was* opened,' Yvonne put in, looking at Cindy. 'Why should he lie?'

'Because he hates Miss Preston, and Mr. Baxter. His mother brought him up to believe that Robert Baxter would treat him as a son and leave him the castle and a good sum of money. When the will was read, Paul was furious. I was not there at the time, but my uncle was. He said he thought the boy would have a fit and that Mrs. Stone was extremely

166

rude and wanted to fight the will, but my uncle persuaded her that she had no hope of winning. Probably the boy said the letter was opened by Miss Preston out of sheer malice.' Keith smiled at Cindy. 'Personally I should have thought that anyone knowing Miss Preston would unhesitatingly believe anything she said.'

'The reporter said she rang him up,' Yvonne chimed in.

Keith looked at her, his eyes narrowed. 'Voices, as doubtless you are aware, can sound very different on the telephone. That sort of evidence would never be accepted in court.'

'But who else would do it? I mean, there's no point in it, is there?' Yvonne asked.

Cindy found her voice. 'But why should *I* do it? All that happened was that I lost the castle.' She stood up, suddenly unable to bear it. 'Excuse me,' she murmured, hurrying out of the room. They were talking about her as if she wasn't there, as if she didn't exist. Why hadn't Peter leapt to her rescue? she wondered. But then, of course, he must be on Yvonne's side. Now who would make up an American buyer?

Suddenly she thought: Mrs. Stone! Knowing the local people, she knew there would be an outcry because their precious Claife Castle was to be demolished and removed to America, another land. Perhaps Mrs. Stone hoped that through the noise and arguments, Cindy's right

167

to the heirdom would be queried, for if the castle was left to her only because she *loved it*—wouldn't her apparent willingness to sell it prove she had no right to have it?

Cindy stayed upstairs as long as she could and then went down, for she didn't want to give them a chance to say anything, and hoped they would all have left the drawing-room. But they hadn't, though Peter and Keith Ayres were obviously making for the library to talk business. Yvonne saw Cindy coming and stood up.

'You do know, of course, Cindy, that your car has been ready in the garage for two days,' she said in her husky voice.

'Two days?' Cindy was startled. 'But I was told it wouldn't be ready until Thursday or Friday.'

'That's your story,' Yvonne said coldly. 'The plain truth is that you intend to stay here as long as you can despite the fact that you should have gone long ago. You have no right to be here.'

Peter looked startled. 'Yvonne, you have no right to say that. I am the host. I asked Cindy to stay. I knew her car was ready, but . . .'

Cindy was suddenly so angry she could hardly speak. She swung round to stare at Peter.

'You knew? Yet you knew very well I wanted to get back to London, and you lied!' she exclaimed angrily.

He smiled and, for a moment, she hated him. He looked so . . . so *complaisant*, which was not a word used generally, though it was one of her boss's favourites.

'For your own good, Cindy. I didn't think it wise for you to start work again so soon after your near-accident. Besides, I knew you loved the castle and I didn't want to deprive you of the pleasure of being here.'

'Oh, you . . . you . . .' She was battling between anger and tears. So she turned to Keith Ayres and caught hold of his arm. 'Would you drive me right away to the garage? I'll pick up my car and I can stay at a hotel. I don't want to be here another moment!'

'Calm down, Cindy,' said Peter, and his condescending voice was the last straw. 'Mr. Ayres and I have business to talk over. You can leave tomorrow morning, but not before. Come along, Ayres,' he said, leading the way.

Cindy rushed by him and stood for a moment on the stairs. 'Please ask Mrs. Stone to bring my dinner up,' she said. 'I never want to speak to either of you again.' She turned and ran up the stairs, stumbling, as the tears ran down her checks.

In her own room, she stood still, her hands to her eyes. How dared he speak like that? As if she was a small child! How dared he lie like that—telling her the car wasn't ready, making it look as if she was the liar, she the one who wanted to stay . . .

169

An hour or so later there was a knock on Cindy's door and she heard Peter's voice.

'Cindy, I want to speak to you,' he said firmly.

She slid off the bed, hastily brushed her hair, and went to the door.

'May I come in?' he asked with that slightly pompous air he put on often and which invariably made her want to laugh.

'It's your castle,' she muttered, standing back.

He came inside, closed the door and looked at her.

'Isn't it time you behaved like an adult and not as a spoilt child?' he asked her.

She was completely taken aback. She wasn't sure what she had expected him to say but it certainly wasn't what he had.

'Why should I stay there and let Yvonne insult me? She implied that I lied about the car and . . .'

He smiled. 'It was me. I apologise, but honestly, Cindy, it was for your good. However, that's the past. We're now involved in the present. I've invited David and Johanna to dinner as I don't want Keith Ayres to be too utterly bored tonight. Somehow he and Yvonne don't hit it off.'

'I'm not surprised,' Cindy said bitterly.

Peter laughed. 'Oh, it's just her way. If you knew her as well as I do, you'd take no notice.' He opened the door. 'You'll be down, then.'

'Yes,' said Cindy, closing the door quickly, leaning against it. Now, why had she agreed? Why should she go and be a sitting duck for Yvonne to aim at? Was she getting like the rest of the females in the Baxter world? A *meek little mouse*, dutifully saying 'Yes', all the time?

She dressed carefully, wearing her long pale green dress with the high waist. It was the only party dress she'd got, for she so seldom went out! But with Yvonne and Johanna looking so beautiful, she had to look her best. At the dinner party, Mrs. Usher had mentioned how well she thought it suited Cindy.

'Charming colour with your hair, my dear.'

A little nervous, Cindy went downstairs. David and Johanna were already there, talking and laughing with Peter over their drinks.

Johanna welcomed her with a smile, but David only with a stiff jerk of his head. Cindy wondered why he disliked her so much. Then Yvonne came in with a flourish, looking ravishing in a shimmering gold maxi-dress.

'David!' she said, holding out both her hands. 'I'm so glad you could come. Peter and Keith will talk shop all the time and one gets so utterly bored.' She flung a quick vague smile at Johanna and ignored Cindy completely.

Dinner was pleasant; as usual, Mrs. Stone had proved what a competent cook she was. Afterwards, as they sat in the drawing-room with coffee and liqueurs, Yvonne sat next to

171

David, as she had done at dinner, talking and laughing with him, while Johanna talked stiffly to Keith and Cindy found herself with Peter.

'I wonder where Roxanna and Martin are,' said Cindy, more for something impersonal to talk about than because she was interested.

'At least the rain is ceasing, so they should start walking soon,' he said casually.

Suddenly he leaned forward, speaking so loudly that automatically everyone looked at him so that there were no longer three groups of two people talking, but one large group.

'Have you heard the latest, Johanna?' he asked with a laugh. 'Yvonne has fallen for the old story about the house with seven chimneys. I think she's even trying to buy it!'

As he spoke he glanced at his cousin David, who immediately looked uncomfortable, fidgeting a little in his chair.

'Well, why not? These legends can't last for years without there being some truth in them,' Yvonne defended herself quickly.

Suddenly Johanna clicked her fingers. 'I've got it!' She looked triumphant and amazingly beautiful in her straight white silk dress. Now her face seemed to glow, her eyes sparkling. 'I remember where I met you!' Johanna pointed a finger at Yvonne. 'It was a few days before Cindy came. You came into my tea-shop and . . .'

'That's absurd, Johanna,' Peter said with a smile. 'Yvonne had never been in the Lake

District before she came straight here.'

Johanna swung round to him. 'Oh yes, I *know* she was here. It was something she said to me that day. You had a blonde wig on,' Johanna said accusingly to the startled Yvonne. 'And you looked fatter and much . . . well, less with it. Also you wore dark glasses. As soon as you started asking questions about Castle Claife I knew you were from the South. I thought what a lot of idiots you must be to believe that after all these years the smugglers' treasure would still be hidden. It so happened I was pretty bored that day, so I played you up. I told you a lot of codswallop about the treasure in the castle that could only be discovered by finding the mysterious path that gave this castle its name. And you said,' Johanna went on triumphantly, 'just as you said just now—that's how I recognised your voice: "These legends couldn't last for years without there being some truth in them." '

Yvonne's face had gone very white, but now her cheeks were flaming with anger.

'You lied to me? Why, you . . . you . . .' she nearly exploded.

Johanna laughed. 'Why not? Only a sucker like you would have fallen, so I laid it on good and thick.'

'You . . . you .' Yvonne half-rose from her chair, looking as if she was going to fly at Johanna in her fury.

Peter spoke quietly, very quietly, so that

173

Cindy's heart seemed to skip a beat.

'You came up here at once to find out about the castle Yvonne? You made up the yarn about the American buyer because you wanted me to claim the castle?'

'Of course I did. It was for you.' Yvonne turned towards him, her face still flushed. 'I had to do something, because you were so stubborn. I came up to see if the castle was worth having. I decided it wasn't because of what it would cost to modernise it. Then this . . . this . . .' she bit back her angry words and glared at Johanna, who was sitting back, her hands folded demurely, her eyes bright with triumph, 'lied to me. I thought when I heard about the treasure that had been hidden for centuries it might be found by modern methods. I thought it worth trying as an investment.'

'You phoned the newspaper to get publicity and make me believe that Cindy was . . .?' Peter began, still with that ominous quietness that made Cindy shiver but that Yvonne didn't seem to notice.

She even smiled. 'Of course I did. I had to do something to make you claim the castle. You were being so impossible, giving away the castle—and perhaps a hidden treasure—to a bit of a girl we didn't even know. The treasure was yours by right and I was determined you should have it. Yes, I wrote the letter which was, unfortunately, delayed. It should have

174

been here before the article in the newspaper. Not my fault. I phoned the newspaper, yes, and it worked,' she went on triumphantly. 'You claimed the castle and . . . and . . .' Her words began to die as she looked at Johanna. 'You . . . you . . .' Yvonne spluttered.

Cindy sat, hunched up, words growing inside her; angry, accusing, ugly words. How could Yvonne be so mean? So greedy, so money-mad? It didn't make sense. It was something she just couldn't understand. It would have been easier to understand if it had been who Cindy had thought: Mrs. Stone. At least she had her love for her son to excuse her. But Yvonne . . .

There was a strange silence in the room. David was leaning back in his chair, arms folded, a dismayed look on his face. Johanna was obviously delighted at the way she had fought her rival. Keith Ayres looked puzzled, glancing from Yvonne to Peter and then back to Yvonne.

It was Peter who spoke first, quietly but so firmly that no one could argue with him. 'This is something we'll discuss tomorrow, Yvonne,' he said coldly. 'Now let's forget it. No one wants to see their dirty washing hanging on the line. Mr. Ayres, I would like you to meet Luke Fairhead tomorrow,' Peter said, his voice conversationally casual as he turned to the solicitor. Then he looked at Johanna. 'It can't be true that you're thinking of selling your tea-shop and leaving us?'

'I was . . . maybe I won't go, now,' said Johanna, looking quickly at David, whose face was flushed as if annoyed.

But Yvonne was not content to leave it at that. She stood up, glared at Johanna and then at Peter.

'A fine way to treat a friend, I must say,' she said angrily. '*I did it for you.* I'll see you in the morning,' she added, and flounced out of the room.

There was another strange silence and then Johanna looked at Peter. 'I'm sorry if I put my foot in it,' she said, her voice sincere. 'It just came out. I had no idea it was Yvonne until she said those same words and I recognised her at once.'

He smiled: a little wearily, Cindy thought.

'Not to worry, Johanna, I had thought it was Yvonne, because I know how crazy she is about making money, but I had no way of proving it. I'm glad it came out this way.'

How brave he was, Cindy was thinking. She longed to comfort him, for how hurt he must be that the girl he loved could behave so meanly. Yet she knew there was nothing she could say. She turned to Keith Ayres, by her side.

'Have you never been here before?' she asked, her voice a little shrill, which startled her. 'It's very lovely.'

Keith Ayres looked at her thoughtfully. 'So

I've heard. You don't mind the rain and the cold?'

Somehow the evening dragged by, with everyone obviously doing his or her best to behave normally, yet undoubtedly the memory of Yvonne Todd, with her flaming cheeks and flashing eyes as she defended herself with the words: 'I did it for you!', could not leave them. At last Peter went outside into the damp night to see Johanna and David off, and Keith was alone with Cindy.

'I'm sorry you should have been involved in all this unpleasantness,' he said in his rather nice, deep voice. 'It must have been an ordeal.'

Cindy shivered. 'It has been. I thought it was Mrs. Stone. I can't understand Yvonne. She's so clever and ...'

'A gambler,' Peter said as he joined them.

Cindy felt her cheeks burn as she looked at him apologetically. 'I ... I ...'

Peter smiled at her. 'That's all right, Cindy. I owe you an apology if anything. Yvonne is a brilliant financier, but her one weakness is gambling. I imagine it's like a disease. Perhaps you'd agree?' Peter turned to Keith Ayres, who nodded.

'Absolutely. The bug bites them and they lose their senses. I can quite see how she felt, though I do rather . . .' Keith hesitated, looking at Cindy.

Peter nodded. 'So do I. Well, Cindy, so you'll be off tomorrow,' he said cheerfully. 'I'll

177

be seeing Yvonne in the morning and then we can have a chat with Luke, but . . .'

'Mr. Ayres will drive me to the garage to pick up my car,' Cindy said quickly. Why prolong the agony? she asked herself, and although she knew the words sounded melodramatic, at least they were the truth. Why did love have to hurt one so? she wondered.

'Good,' said Peter, still cheerful. 'See you in the morning,' he said, and walked towards the library, looking back. 'I wonder if you could spare me a moment here, Ayres. It might be an idea if we looked at these figures now, save time in the morning. I know Cindy is eager to get off.'

Cindy went upstairs slowly. It meant nothing to Peter that tomorrow she was going. Really, this time! Alone in her room, she looked at Uncle Robert's diary. Should she hand it to Peter tomorrow? Would he impatiently toss it aside? Would it have more weight with him if it came by post, together with an explanatory letter? she wondered. He could be so impatient at times, he might not give her a chance to tell him what he had to know.

The door handle turned. Hastily she tucked the book under her pillow and wondered if she had done it fast enough as Mrs. Stone appeared, a hot water bottle in her hand. Every night she put a bottle in each bed, but surely tonight she was rather late?

'It's very good of you, Mrs. Stone,' said Cindy, uncomfortably aware that Mrs. Stone was looking at her curiously. This wasn't the first time Mrs. Stone had nearly caught her reading Uncle Robert's notes, Cindy realised. Anyhow, only tonight left, she comforted herself. This time tomorrow she would be miles away . . .

Alone. Alone in her miserable little bedsitter. How was she going to bear it?

Simple, she told herself as she quickly undressed. She had no choice. It was as simple as that.

CHAPTER TWELVE

In the morning Cindy found only Keith in the dining-room. Mrs. Stone was telling him that Mr. Baxter and Miss Todd had gone off some time before—and that Miss Todd had taken all her luggage with her. This, Mrs. Stone said almost triumphantly, and she glanced silently at Cindy as if thinking: 'Well, she'll be gone soon, too!'

As they ate the well-cooked bacon and eggs, Keith Ayres looked at Cindy.

'I think you took it very well yesterday. Most girls would have been furious with Miss Todd.'

Cindy smiled. 'I was—terribly angry. There were lots of things I wanted to say, but what was the good? The damage was done.'

'I still think you're being very generous. The castle would have been yours all right. Peter Baxter didn't want it.'

Cindy poured out some more coffee. 'I'm afraid you were right, you know.' She sighed. 'I had a long talk with Mr. Fairhead—you'll like him, a very nice man—and quite honestly, I don't know *how* I was going to keep the castle going, so maybe it's better this way. At least Uncle Robert would be happy knowing Peter was here.'

Keith Ayres passed her the toast, then the butter and marmalade. 'Mrs. Stone is a good cook.'

'Isn't she?' Cindy gave a little laugh. 'I had a feeling that it was Mrs. Stone who'd told the newspaper all those lies. I never once thought of Yvonne.'

'It's certainly more understandable from Mrs. Stone's point of view,' Keith Ayres agreed. He glanced at her thoughtfully. 'Is it true, Miss Preston, that you're in love with your boss?'

'In love with my boss?' Cindy was startled. 'What makes you ask that?'

'Just that Peter Baxter is rather annoyed because you're so eager to get back to London. He said you were crazy about your boss.'

Cindy laughed. 'Of course I'm not! I only said he was a good thoughtful boss and I liked him. Peter jumped to conclusions, that's all.'

'I see.' He smiled. 'Then you're not bespoken for.'

'Goodness, no,' Cindy said quickly, and wished Keith Ayres would not look at her so intently. She began to twirl a spoon on the tablecloth, concentrating on it.

'Not by anyone?' Keith Ayres asked quietly.

'Not by anyone.' After all, that was the truth, Cindy thought. She loved Peter, but that didn't mean he loved her!

'I wonder when he'll be back.' Keith Ayres sounded impatient. 'I want to get to London and I know you do, too. I wonder if it might be a good idea to go and get your car now.'

'Oh no,' Cindy said quickly. 'Peter will have arranged for you to meet Luke Fairhead and he . . . well, he would be annoyed if you weren't here when he got back. It sounds as if he was driving Yvonne to the station, but it wouldn't surprise me in the least if she comes back with him.'

'You think he'd let her?'

Cindy shrugged. 'They're always quarrelling. You should hear them, and the next moment, smiling at one another. It's just the sort of quarrelling some married people seem to enjoy.'

'For the making it up again?' he suggested.

'Yes.'

'So you think they'll . . . marry?'

Shrugging again, Cindy said: 'I honestly don't know. She seems to think so. She said they would only live up here a part of the year, but usually they'd be in London.'

'And he—what did he say?'

'Oh, he wasn't there. He's never said anything about marriage, but he's . . . well, I would say he is in love with her, because he lets her nag him and he finds it funny. Now if I tried to do that . . .'

'He wouldn't find it funny?'

'He'd tell me to stop acting like a child,' Cindy said ruefully.

They finished breakfast and went to stand outside the castle. The sun was not out, but at least it was not raining. Cindy waved her hand towards the lake.

'Isn't it beautiful?'

Keith Ayres gave her a quick look. 'You'll miss it. Very different from London's traffic and noise.'

'I know,' Cindy said wistfully. 'However, I do get out in the country at weekends. Having a car makes that easy.'

They walked towards the cliff edge where the grass slid down towards the water, and turned to look at the castle.

'I must confess,' Keith Ayres said slowly, 'to me it's just a castle—a big one and in good condition, admittedly, but all the same a *mock* castle. No history, nothing to make it stand out.'

'But it's beautiful!' Cindy turned to him. 'Don't you love all those towers and the funny chimneys at the back and . . . and . . .'

'Everything? You love it because it was a childhood dream. I think we all remember certain times when we were very happy when young.'

Cindy didn't answer for a moment. She was staring at the castle, taking in the beauty of the battlements, the aged drawbridge, the water that still trickled through what had once been the moat. How many times must she say goodbye to the castle? she wondered sadly, for each time it was harder than before.

A car came up the drive. They turned and saw Peter, who waved, and as soon as he was out of the car, came striding across to them. He looked pleased with life.

'Here I am. Sorry to have kept you waiting,' he said cheerfully. Then he looked at Cindy and his voice changed. 'I imagine you'll want to pack. You can have your chauffeur in an hour's time. Come on, Ayres, Luke will be waiting for us.'

The two men walked away. Cindy looked up at the majestic façade of the castle once again and then went into the hall and up to her room. She finished packing, locked the suitcase and took it down to the hall. Then she went into the library to look through the many books in order to pass the time. She found one that interested her—it was to do with the future of castles and questioned how much longer castles would be protected and paid for by the State.

Curled up on the window seat, Cindy was reading this when she heard a noise in the hall. She began to get up and then sat back, for it was probably Mrs. Stone polishing the beautifully-carved banister and Cindy was in no mood for Mrs. Stone's icy glare.

When Cindy heard the men's voices in the hall she hurried to join them. They were talking seriously, but both smiled as they saw her.

'A cup of coffee,' Peter said cheerfully, 'and then you can be on your way. I've phoned the garage, Cindy, and the car is ready for you.

Luckily not too much damage was done. I'll just tell Mrs. Stone . . .'

'No, I will,' Cindy said, and ran down the hall to the baize door that shut off the kitchen area. 'Mrs. Stone!' she called, and heard a drawer slam. Mrs. Stone came to meet her, her face flushed, her hair more wispy than usual.

'What is it now?' she asked crossly.

'Mr. Baxter would like coffee for the three of us, please,' Cindy said, and hurried back to the men, who were still talking in the drawing-room.

The coffee came—delicious, as usual, and very hot. As they drank it, Cindy listened to the two men discussing the castle's finances.

'Admittedly it means a good deal would have to be invested, but I agree that it should pay in the long run. It could be the sort of hotel that would attract tourists.' Keith Ayres grinned. 'Why not ask Miss Younge to be receptionist? Her tales of hidden treasure might encourage even more visitors!'

A cloud seemed to pass over Peter's face, but it was soon gone. 'A good idea—if she stays here. I think she's getting rather fed up with life.'

'She's lonely,' said Cindy.

Keith Ayres turned at once. 'Aren't we all? I don't know about you, Miss Preston, but I reckon one of the loneliest places in the world is a bed-sitter in London.'

Cindy nodded. 'I should know,' she agreed.

185

'I'd have thought you'd make friends more easily here.'

'I agree all the way,' said Peter, 'but it might not be friends who talk your language, share your interests. I think that's the trouble with Johanna. She feels she's growing old before her time. Maybe a difficult job in London would boost her morale a bit. She's still a very attractive person.'

Everyone was attractive to Peter except herself, Cindy thought unhappily. Keith Ayres, glancing at his watch, stood up.

'I'll just go up to my room and check that I've left nothing out. I see your suitcase is already down,' he said to Cindy.

'Yes.'

And then they were alone, she and Peter. Peter stirred his coffee slowly, looking intently at it.

Suddenly Cindy could bear it no more. Poor Peter, he was so miserable and so bravely hiding it.

'I'm sorry about Yvonne,' she said gently. 'Some people are made like that.'

Peter looked up. 'Don't be sorry for her, Cindy, she needs a good spanking. It was the meanest, most disgusting trick to play. And all because she wants more money. She's already incredibly wealthy. She inherited a fortune from her grandfather.'

'I . . .' Cindy hesitated, but she had to know. 'Are you going to marry her?'

'What? Me?' Peter was obviously amazed. 'What on earth made you think that?'

Cindy twirled a spoon, avoiding his eyes. 'She . . . she told me that you . . . well, she said "we" will only live here part of the year.'

'Yvonne was always implying that we should marry, but no . . . my word, Cindy, imagine being married to her!' He laughed suddenly. 'I wouldn't wish it on my worst enemy. I've known her for years, met her in Australia first. We always seem to be meeting, by chance— that is, by chance where I'm concerned. I sometimes wondered if she wasn't there with a purpose. You see, her father's a stockbroker and she's really good about stocks and shares and advises me. Marriage? Never!' he said scornfully.

He stood up, as if eager to be rid of her, Cindy thought, so she stood up, too. Then Peter startled her as he said, almost wistfully, 'I just wish Dad knew that I was doing what he wanted me to do . . .'

She knew in that moment that Peter was in a receptive mood.

'Peter,' she said, catching hold of his arm, 'will you promise to let me say something without jumping down my throat or telling me to grow up?'

He looked amused. 'Okay, but what's it all about?'

'Your father, Peter. Please . . . please don't interrupt. I'll be as quick as I can, but . . . but you must let me tell you,' she said breathlessly, unaware that she was clinging to his arm. 'I found your father's diary in a secret drawer in his desk. Maybe I shouldn't have read it, but I wondered what sort of a man he was. Peter, he never got *one* of your letters. He kept saying in the notes that if only you would write a few lines to let him know you were well . . . That time you came to see him, he was ill. Not very, but Mrs. Stone refused to let him have visitors, he said she fussed and he was lonely, but he was too tired to fight her. Peter, I believe Mrs. Stone kept those letters from your father, that it was she who told you to get out and not your father at all.' Cindy stopped, completely breathless as she stared at the man standing silent by her side.

'You've got the diary?' he asked gruffly, his face looking grave.

'Yes, in my suitcase. I've got the key here. I was afraid you wouldn't listen to me. I've made notes of the dates to look at, because your father wrote terribly small and it's hard to read . . . I was so afraid your impatience would make you toss it on one side, but you should read it, you must . . .'

'Well, let's get it.'

They went to the hall. Cindy bent over the suitcase, then looked up, her face startled. 'The lock's been broken!'

Peter bent down by her side to look at it. 'Been forced open,' he said curtly. 'We'd better

188

see Mrs. Stone.'

Keith Ayres came down the stairs. 'Trouble?' he enquired.

'It seems Cindy found some notes my father had written and she thought I should read them. She left them in here, but the lock's been broken.'

'Better make sure they're not inside.'

Cindy looked up. 'They won't be.' She was nearly in tears. It was so terribly important that Peter should see his father's words, to know his father had forgiven him and wanted to be forgiven in turn. However, she opened the suitcase. 'I left them on the top.'

They weren't there!

Peter was down the hall in a moment, Cindy hurried after him, Keith Ayres close behind.

Mrs. Stone was stirring a saucepan on the stove and looked startled to see the three of them coming out.

'You want some coffee now? she asked.

'No, Mrs. Stone,' Peter said quietly. 'I want my father's diary.'

'Your father's diary? What's t'do with me? I don't know anything about your father's notes,' she said.

'The lock on Miss Preston's suitcase in the hall has been broken and the diary taken out.'

Mrs. Stone looked indignant. 'She's accusing me, is she now? Well, maybe you'd better look at her. No doubt she broke the lock so that she could accuse me and make trouble.'

'Mrs. Stone,' Peter said even more quietly, 'this is a serious matter. Did you or did you not break open Miss Preston's suitcase and remove a book?'

'I . . . did . . . not!' Mrs. Stone almost shouted.

Suddenly Cindy remembered something. When she had hurried out to Mrs. Stone to ask her for some coffee, she'd heard a drawer slam.

'Peter,' she said, 'it's in one of the drawers.'

She knew she was right, for Mrs Stone's face turned almost purple. 'You've got no right t'open the drawers. They're my private property!'

'They are not, you know,' Keith Ayres said gently. 'We have every right to look in them.'

'You . . . Mr. Baxter, now, it's not fair . . .' Mrs. Stone waved a wooden spoon at them. 'Never before has anyone accused me of theft!'

'Mrs. Stone,' Cindy felt she could no longer hold her tongue, 'you didn't want those notes read because you knew Mr. Baxter would say he'd never received a letter, nor did he ever know his son had been to see him.'

Mrs. Stone's cheeks were bright red now, her eyes flashing vindictively. 'Ever since you came here, you've tried t'cause trouble, any time. I am not a liar nor a thief, and I . . .'

'Careful, Mrs. Stone,' said Keith Ayres, turning from a drawer in the dresser. 'I've

190

found the diary!'

He handed the long flat book to Peter, who opened it, frowning a little as he saw the tiny neat print, then unfolded a piece of paper. 'You worked hard on this, Cindy,' he said. 'It means a lot to you?'

'I want you to know that your father did love you,' she said earnestly. 'It's so terrible when you feel no one loves you.'

He turned to Mrs. Stone. 'Did you send the letters back to me, Mrs. Stone? Was it a lie when you told me my father never wanted to see me again?' He patted the book in his hands. 'I have the evidence here.'

It was as if something exploded in Mrs. Stone, for suddenly she was screaming at him.

'Of course I did! I had to keep you away from him. 'Twasn't fair, and that's the truth, you go off to live your own life and I look after him—then up you turn and expect to start again. What about the work I did? What about my son Paul? A proper son to the old man, he was. And what do I get for my ten years' work? A paltry thousand quid and nothing for my poor Paul who'd been a-counting on it . . . I had to think of Paul, and I knew you didn't really care . . .'

Peter took Cindy by the arm and bent, whispering to her.

'Please go, Cindy, I'd rather handle this on my own. Look after this, though.' He gave her the diary.

191

She obeyed and went to stand in the drawing-room by the french window, looking through blurred eyes at the serene blue lake below. The sun had thrust the clouds on one side, the distant mountains were almost blue in the strange light. Poor Mrs. Stone, Cindy was thinking. It was understandable when Mrs. Stone loved her only child so much. Cindy hoped Peter would be charitable.

When the two men rejoined her, she saw that Peter was the cheerful one.

'Don't look so worried, Cindy,' he said. 'I'll see that she's looked after financially. They'll have to go, of course, but I'll give her a good reference.'

'But what will you do?' Cindy's eyes widened with dismay. 'You can't cook and clean the castle, Peter.'

He laughed, 'Not to worry, Cindy. I have friends. Probably Luke's wife will come and lend a hand or find someone from the village. It'll be better without the Stones on the property, she gives me the creeps and he makes me want to box his cheeky ears.' He smiled as he turned to Keith Ayres. 'Sorry to land you in my domestic troubles like this.' He took the book from Cindy. 'Thanks, Cindy, for going to so much trouble. I'll read every word if it takes me the rest of my life,' he promised with a smile.

'I found a magnifying glass helpful. I've got one in my suitcase.'

'There's one in the library, thanks. Well,' Peter looked at them both, 'you want to be on your way, I suppose. Let's take the luggage out to the car. One thing, the weather is good.'

Silently Cindy followed as Peter carried her suitcase. She gave one last look round the huge lofty hall, and then walked across the gravel to the car, trying not to look back at the castle but failing at the last moment. She stared up at it as it towered above her. The castle where she had known both sadness and happiness. She would never forget it, she knew that.

'Cindy,' Peter urged, and she looked round. He was standing by the car, holding the door open. She realised with a shock that he was eager to get rid of them.

'Thanks,' she said as she got in by Keith Ayres' side.

Peter closed the door, tested it to make sure it was shut, then spoke through the window. 'You won't forget the research you promised to do for me, Cindy?'

His face was so near and yet so far. Her hand ached as she fought the longing just to stroke his cheek once. The tears seemed to be gathering, but she managed a watery smile.

'I won't forget, Peter,' she said, and as the car moved forward, she added quietly, 'Anything.'

'A nasty business for Peter Baxter,' Keith Ayres observed as the track neared the main road.

'Horrible,' Cindy agreed, grateful that he had kept silent for so long. She had fought and overcome the desire to look back at the castle. After all, she didn't really need to look at it—she had only to close her eyes and she could see it again, with all its mock-majesty. In a way it was a farce, something to make people laugh. Just as her love for Peter was . . . a farce.

'Poor Mrs. Stone,' she sighed. 'She only wants to help Paul.'

'Actually she's doing the worst thing she can do for the boy. He's a cheeky layabout, that's all. Do him good to have to work.'

'But will he ever work?'

'That's her problem. Tell me, what do you think of Peter Baxter?' Keith Ayres asked suddenly.

'Peter? Well, I like him . . . very much,' Cindy said without thinking. 'Don't you?' She turned to look at her companion.

'I do and I don't,' he said as they turned off the track on to the main road. 'He's either extremely self-disciplined or very callous. He seems to take everything in his stride—his girl-friend's behaviour, the housekeeper who hurt his father so much by holding back those letters and not letting the old man see his son . . . yet Peter Baxter . . . well, I don't know what to make of him.'

'He told me he wasn't in love with Yvonne.

He said there was nothing like that—just that they've known one another for years and she advised him about stocks and shares.'

'I gathered she was very bright. Honestly, though, how she fell for that tale about treasure in the castle! I suppose that once a gambler, always a gambler. You say you like Peter Baxter. He seems to like you. He's paying all your expenses for your trip up here. I've been given instructions to send you a substantial cheque.'

What was Peter doing? Cindy thought unhappily. Paying her off? 'There's no need for him to do that.'

'There is. The estate would have paid your expenses anyhow. I just wondered how you saw him.'

'Well, it's difficult,' Cindy said slowly. 'He's kind and thoughtful and yet he can be very cruel. He was always saying I was so young and a child and . . .'

'I suppose to a man of thirty-three, a girl of nineteen is rather young.'

'I suppose so,' Cindy said miserably. 'Almost a different generation.'

'He's very . . . well, let's say authoritative. I suppose he's been in executive positions?'

'I don't know, really. He's an engineer, and has been in Africa, Australia, Canada, practically everywhere.'

'Somehow I can't see him settling down to a cabbage existence in the castle.'

195

'Why should that be a cabbage existence?' Cindy asked quickly.

Keith Ayres shrugged. 'Sooner him than me. The countryside is lovely, but . . .'

'But . . .?' Cindy was almost aggressive at the thought of anyone attacking her beloved Lakeland.

'What sort of people will he meet? The Fairheads . . . but they're years older. Of course there's always Johanna,' Keith Ayres chuckled. 'Maybe she'll get her fangs in him now Miss Todd is away.'

'Johanna is in love with David.'

'But David is obviously not in love with Johanna,' Keith Ayres said with equal haste. 'So where will Johanna look now?'

Cindy was glad they had reached the garage then so that she need not answer. But it was the seed of a thought he had tossed into her brain, a seed that was to grow with alarming speed in the next few days.

She could see her little grey car waiting for her and pointed it out to her companion. He looked rather amused.

'You won't want me driving on your tail all the time, so I suggest we meet for lunch. I'll drive ahead and book a table.' He told her the name of the place he suggested and of a good hotel he knew there.

'If you don't turn up,' he promised, 'I'll come and look for you.'

'I shall be all right,' she said stiffly.

He smiled. 'I'm sure you will, but at the moment you're a little trouble-prone. Everything you have to do with seems to go wrong.'

How right he was, Cindy thought as she watched the large dark green car pull out and she went to find the garage owner.

'What do I owe you?' she asked him, a little nervous, for she was afraid it might be more than the cash she had with her.

'Nothing, miss,' the manager, a tall, thin man with a cap pulled over one eye, smiled. 'Mr. Baxter, he paid for it.'

'Oh!' Cindy frowned. 'It's . . . it's all right now?'

'Fine . . . goes like t'little bomb, it does any time,' the man told her with a smile.

Driving along the roads, Cindy had little time to think, yet at the back of her mind gnawed several unhappy thoughts. Peter's obvious eagerness to get rid of them. Who was he expecting? Had he merely left Yvonne somewhere and promised to fetch her back when the others were safely out of the way? Or was it Johanna? Keith Ayres' suggestion was growing fast in her mind. Peter had obviously liked Johanna . . . and Johanna? Caught on the rebound, it was easy to mistake liking for love.

Cindy was quite relieved when she reached the hotel Keith had told her about and he was waiting for her. There was no doubt but that he was a very nice man. She felt so relaxed when she was with him, for he talked interestingly and made her laugh a lot.

They were having coffee when Keith took her breath away, without warning, as he said abruptly:

'It's Peter, isn't it?'

To Cindy's horror, the tears stung her eyes. She nodded silently. Keith leaned forward and put his hand over hers.

'You poor darling,' he said tenderly.

CHAPTER THIRTEEN

Cindy's return to London was like a nightmare. Her small, square bed-sitter with its narrow bed, curtained corner that was a wardrobe, a small table and chair and the dismal lime-green curtains was such a contrast to the huge rooms of the castle that she found herself constantly comparing them. She realised she had also been spoilt, taking it for granted her meals would be prepared, whereas now she forgot her evening meal and did no shopping.

She couldn't have returned at a worse time, for after she and Keith Ayres had parted after lunch, they ran into rain and the last part of her journey was a miserable one with the rain pounding down mercilessly. There was, of course, no one to greet her after she had parked her little car and carried her suitcase back down the Place where her bed-sitter was on the fourth floor. Somehow, that evening, she missed the welcome she had never known before her stay at the castle. It was so still, not even Mrs. Craddock, her landlady, in sight as Cindy trudged up the steep narrow staircase, her suitcase dragging her back. Then she opened the door and the awful dull impersonality of the room hit her.

She closed the door, leaning against it,

looking round at the smallness. There was no possible way of calling it 'home'. She knew, though, that it was mostly her own fault. She had wanted to save up for a car so much that nothing else mattered; hence she was paying as low a rent as she could, nor had she spent money on bright posters or gay bed-covers as others did. She shuddered at the thought of what Peter would say if he ever saw this dingy cell, for that was what it was. The cell in which she was a prisoner . . .

Hastily she unpacked. Realising she had no food, she unearthed a box of water biscuits and some honey and made herself a cup of coffee. An early night would be a good idea.

But was it? She tossed and turned in the narrow bed, moving quickly several times and nearly falling out! Sleep was far away. No matter how hard she tried to push the castle and Peter out of her thoughts, they returned again and again, refusing to be forgotten.

How kind Keith Ayres had been, she thought, grateful for a different thought. She had nearly cried, but after he had comforted her, he had changed the subject and even made her laugh. Was it so obvious? Cindy found herself wondering anxiously. If Keith Ayres could see her love for Peter so plainly, then could . . . ?

She squirmed in the narow bed. Was that why Peter was so eager to see them go? Why, he had almost pushed them out of the castle.

Because he thought she was *after* him!

Tears finally helped her and she fell asleep with her checks wet. In the morning, she awoke and faced the truth. She had to accept it! There was nothing else she could do.

She had a warm welcome at the office on Monday when she began work, the girls crowding round to hear what had happened. Cindy hesitated about telling them everything, for she had no desire to cause more trouble.

'The real heir, Mr. Baxter's son, was found,' she explained simply.

But the girls weren't prepared to leave it at that.

'What about that article in the papers? Were you really going to get twenty thousand pounds for the castle?' Maggie asked eagerly.

'I knew nothing about that until someone showed me the paper,' Cindy could say truthfully. 'It was all a hoax.'

Maggie looked disappointed. 'You mean it wasn't true? There wasn't an American?'

'No, someone did it for a . . .'

'Joke? Funny kind of joke,' Maggie declared, and Cindy silently agreed with her.

Yvonne's 'joke' had lost Cindy the castle; yet Cindy knew in her heart that she could never have kept the castle, for how could she, a girl of nineteen, ever raise the money required? It was different for a man of Peter's age and finances.

Mr. Jenkins was more discerning. As he

dictated the letters, he sighed and Cindy looked up. Her boss's face was grave.

'Miss Preston,' he said slowly, 'I see you have your glasses on today, so that can't be used as an excuse. What have you in mind?'

Cindy's forehead wrinkled as she stared at him. 'I . . . what . . . what have I in mind?'

He nodded. 'Yes, what excuse today have you for the fact that I've dictated for ten minutes and you haven't done a single one of those little squiggles you seem so efficient in reading back,' he said drily.

Cindy looked at her notebook in dismay. He was right. She had neither heard nor realised she wasn't listening. She had been thinking of Peter . . . wondering how he was managing with no Mrs. Stone there. Had Johanna taken him under her wing, or was it Mrs. Fairhead?

'I'm sorry,' she said sincerely.

Mr. Jenkins gave an odd smile. 'That's good of you. So am I. Before you went to see your castle, Miss Preston, you were extremely on edge, making foolish mistakes that were unlike you, but which I forgave as I know what heartache can do. Then this excitement about the mock castle and off you go, thrilled. Now you come back, even less aware of what's going on around you than before. We seem to be back to Square One. Just what has happened? You've fallen in love?'

'Yes,' Cindy admitted.

'I see. And he?'

'Sees me as a child and . . . and . . .'

Mr Jenkins smiled. 'Well, it's hard not to, Miss Preston. I suppose you'll get over it if I bear with you?'

Cindy blinked. 'Of course. I have no choice.'

'Very sensible of you, Miss Preston. I suggest you type the letters you've got down and maybe tomorrow you'll be feeling better. Meanwhile send Maggie in to me, she can do the rest of the letters.'

'Yes, Mr. Jenkins.' Gratefully Cindy escaped to her little office, pausing to tell Miss Point what Mr. Jenkins had said.

That night Cindy went home, having been to the supermarket and bought a 'meal in a bag' that she could heat up on her gas ring. Her depression was, if anything, greater than ever. The drabness of the room seemed even more stark than before. How could she bear to go on living in this . . . this . . . She couldn't find a word to describe it.

As her dinner slowly cooked, she read the evening paper, not really reading, her eyes skimming over the words because it was better to do something than just sit there and think.

It was the word *America* that caught her eye and made her start to really read the short article about an employment agency which made a speciality of finding efficient British secretaries for jobs in the States. The pay was good, though the qualifications demanded were high.

Was that the answer? Cindy wondered. It was unusual for her to buy an evening paper—why had she done so that night? Was it to show her a way to escape? A completely new life, different people, a challenge to her?

Wouldn't that be wiser than sitting here in this . . . this . . . and fretting? Surely the only way to overcome painful memories was to lead so busy a life you had no time to sit and mope? she asked herself.

She made a note of the name and address of the agency. Would she have time to go in her lunch hour? she wondered. Or perhaps they weren't open at that time? She decided to write to them and ask when it would be convenient to call.

One thing, Mr. Jenkins would give her a good reference, she knew that, and maybe he would be glad to see her go if he was finding her, as he said, 'not with it' at the moment. She wrote several letters before she was satisfied with one. Maybe she should have typed it, she thought. Yet she could remember Mr. Jenkins saying that the best way to read a person's character was to look at their handwriting! Cindy studied hers worriedly, and then went over the spelling carefully. Luckily, she thought, she was a natural speller.

She addressed the envelope and sealed it. In the lunch hour next day she'd get a stamp and post it.

Her dinner was bubbling fiercely. She only

204

hoped it was not overdone. Eating it, she found herself looking ahead . . . Suppose she was sent to New York? What would it be like? Salaries were very high there, but so was the cost of living, she reminded herself, but it would be nice to meet new people.

She pushed the empty plate on one side, flung herself down on her bed and wept. There was one person she could not fool. Herself!

Next day she was determinedly bright at the office. Mr. Jenkins made no comments, but she got through all his letters in record time. In the lunch hour she posted the letter to the employment agency.

It was absurd how miserable she felt. Yet she knew she was doing the right thing. If you couldn't overcome pain, ignore it; fill your life so full, she told herself sternly.

Mr. Jenkins sent for her that afternoon.

'Miss Preston, full marks for your behaviour today,' he said with a smile. She smiled back. 'Now as a reward, how about having dinner with me tonight?'

She was really startled. Perhaps it showed in her face, because he chuckled.

'My eldest daughter is about your age. She's meeting me with her latest boy-friend. I thought four would be a more comfortable group than three.'

'It's very kind of you,' Cindy began, and suddenly knew she could not go. Mr. Jenkins' eldest daughter and her latest boy-friend, both probably looking gooey-eyed at one another, which would only make everything much worse. 'I'd love to, but . . . but I have a date.'

Mr. Jenkins smiled. 'Good—so long as you're not sitting at home alone weeping. It makes your eyes swell, you know.'

'Does it?' Cindy's hand flew to her glasses.

Back at her desk, she was busy filing when the phone rang. It was a private call for her.

Peter, she thought instantly, her heart seeming to leap with joy.

But it wasn't. It was Keith Ayres.

'How are things going, Cindy?' he asked, his voice concerned. 'I guess it must be pretty tough.' Actually he had told her at the lunch they shared that he felt guilty about her unhappiness and that he should have waited until the three years were up before telling her of the castle.

Cindy managed a little laugh. 'It's not exactly easy, Keith, but . . .'

'I know. Look, I've got tickets for a concert at the Festival Hall and wondered if you'd care to come.'

Music! Cindy swallowed. That would be the last straw. She could just see herself, sitting by Keith's side, the tears running down her cheeks. If anything could make her cry, it was music.

'I'm awfully sorry, but I've got a date,' she lied.

'I see. Another time?' he spoke cheerfully

206

and she wondered if he knew she wasn't telling the truth. 'Be seeing you,' he added, and rang off.

She put down the telephone slowly. Was she being stupid? she asked herself. Should she have accepted one of the invitations? It was no good, just sitting in that awful little room . . . Funny, because until she'd been to the castle, the little room hadn't seemed awful—it was as if the castle and Peter had changed her entire outlook on life.

On the way home, she was tempted to go to a cinema, yet felt that would be just as bad. Just give herself a few days and everything would be better, she tried to comfort herself.

The hall door was always left unlocked. She walked up the steep stairs wearily, thinking of the long lonely hours ahead, and then, as she turned the corner for her last flight, she stopped dead.

It couldn't be true, she thought. It must be a dream. But it wasn't.

Peter was sitting on the stairs, reading a newspaper. He must have heard her gasp, for he put it down and smiled at her.

'Hullo,' he said cheerfully.

'But . . . Peter . . . what are you doing here?' And then she understood. Or thought she did. 'I'm afraid I haven't had time to do any research yet,' she added.

He folded the paper neatly, stood up and came down the stairs to stand on the small landing by her side.

'I came to ask you to dinner,' he said with a smile. Just as if it was the most natural thing in the world, Cindy thought. Somehow it riled her, so she lifted her chin.

'That's funny—you're the third man today who's asked me out,' she told him.

'Is that so?' Peter began to laugh. 'Looks as if I'm a bit late. Some other time?' He began to turn away and she knew she couldn't do it.

'I said no to the others,' she almost whispered.

Peter nodded as he turned back. 'I'm glad. I'm really here,' he went on, lightly chatting, 'to fight your boss. I admit it's hardly fair, for you haven't been working until nine-thirty tonight, nor will we, I hope, both spend the evening yawning.' It was his pompous tone she knew so well and loved. As usual it made her laugh.

'I'd better change,' she began.

He looked her up and down thoughtfully, at the white laced boots, the unbuttoned long green coat, the little matching hat perched on her chestnut-brown hair that hung to her shoulders.

'I like you as you are,' he said lightly, taking her arm. 'Come on. No wonder you're slim, climbing up and down these stairs so often!'

His car was parked close by. As usual it was difficult to find a parking place in the West End, but he finally succeeded, as he always succeeded, Cindy thought. She hardly talked, glad to leave it to him, yet all the time she was wondering what this was all about. Why had he driven all this way to take her out to dinner? Was he feeling guilty? Was this to be a compensation for Yvonne's behaviour? Or was he just being kind?

Despite her tenseness and her knowledge that being with him like this would only make it worse when the parting came again, Cindy enjoyed the evening. A good dinner, then dancing.

She had never been in Peter's arms before. He was much taller than she was, so she was not tempted to put her cheek against his! He danced the old way and actually she preferred it; perhaps because it meant she was in his arms, she thought, and could fool herself for a while.

The evening fled by with Cindy wishing it would not end, and then Peter took her back to the bed-sitter. In the hall, he looked down at her.

'Well?' he asked.

'Well?' she echoed, puzzled.

'Was I as kind and thoughtful as him?'

'As who?'

Peter chuckled. 'Your boss, of course. You were always praising him. Was I? I mean, how am I as a rival? Have I any hope?'

Cindy was tired and suddenly not in a mood for jokes.

'A hope of what?' she asked crossly.

Peter took hold of her shoulders and looked down at her. 'Have I a hope of being a more suitable husband than your beloved boss?'

She stared up at him. Her throat seemed to tighten, her nose prickled. How could he be so cruel, taunting her? she wondered.

'Is this some kind of a joke?' she asked angrily.

'A joke?' Peter sounded shocked. 'Look, Cindy, I knew your boss meant a lot to you. I could tell that from the way you wanted to get back to London, but then . . . well, after you'd gone, it was so quiet and lonely and I had time to think. It was then I realised just how stupid I'd been. Maybe it was seeing Caterina, the gipsy, who reminded me of the family curse. I think I told you about it? That the family would never be free of the curse until the castle owner's wife ceased to be a meek little mouse. I realised then that *I* was acting like a meek little mouse.'

Cindy found herself laughing, for he looked so odd, so solemn. 'You—a meek little mouse? Oh, Peter!'

'I mean it.' He didn't even smile. 'I asked myself why I had been willing to accept the fact that you loved your boss. Why hadn't I asked you. So here I am. Cindy, do you love your boss?'

'Of course I don't! I never did.' Cindy was getting confused again. What did Peter mean?

He couldn't . . . ?

But it seemed he could, for he suddenly put his arms round her, his face near hers as he said quietly:

'Then you mean—? There is some hope for me?'

'Oh, Peter!' Maddeningly the tears slid down her cheeks, but Peter took no notice.

'You really mean?' he asked, his arms tightening round her.

'Of course I do. It was always you,' Cindy told him. Now her arms were round his neck, her cheek against his. 'Peter—I just can't believe it.'

'Neither can I,' he said, and kissed her.